The Priso

C000089354

Experiences of a Teacher in a Male Prison

Krysia Martin

chipmunkapublishing

the mental health publisher

Published by

Chipmunkapublishing

PO Box 6872

Brentwood

Essex CM13 1ZT

United Kingdom

http://www.chipmunkapublishing.com

Chipmunkapublishing gratefully acknowledge the support of Arts Council England.

"Education is not the filling of a pail, but the lighting of a fire"

W.B Yeats

All the names in the stories have been changed and so have some of the lesser details.

Krysia Martin

PART ONE

THE PRISON TEACHER

Krysia Martin

She managed to park her car in the prison car park. It was full to bursting, so she squeezed herself into a tiny spot, locked away her mobile phone and walked up the wide driveway.

The white prison glowed in the sunlight, with its two flags, the Union Jack and the Prison Service, hanging limply on their poles. It was going to be hot, with no wind to ease the temperature. It was going to be hot in the classroom. She hoped that no other department had pinched the fan.

She passed through the main gate, showed her pass, and picked up her keys almost robotically, her mind elsewhere. The gate officers cracked a joke, and she smiled at them.

Inside, there was a different world. It was darker somehow, in shadow, far away from the heat and bright sunlight outside. She walked up the steps, pushed open the main door, and walked up the white admin corridor. People were coming in with her. Officers in their smart uniforms were striding briskly to their wings, Governors, "suits", were stopping to chat, as she walked on. She opened the gate into the Centre, and the four wings spread out before her.

It was noisy. She heard the clanging of cell doors as the officers unlocked the prisoners for work. Men in their grey or maroon uniforms were appearing from their cells, sleepily rubbing their eyes, or moving smartly towards the showers and the hot water. It was noisy. People were surprised at the noise when they visited, used to television pictures of quiet wings and landings, when prisoners were locked away so that their faces could not be caught on camera. Now, prisoners were shouting to each other, officers were calling out. Shouts of "Educa..shun", "Let's have you for Educa..shun"..., clanging of doors, keys jangling, gates banging. Not a quiet place, a prison.

She unlocked the gate to the wing, and walked up the landing. The prisoners greeted her cheerfully, "Hullo Miss!", "How are you?" "You look nice." "Gonna be a scorcher". She smiled at them. Despite the surroundings, the noise and the clamour, the prisoners made her work worthwhile. As she walked up the landing, some came up, asking her questions about the class, or proudly telling her about some achievement – "Miss, I found the name of that …", "Miss, when am I going to get on classes?" or joking, "Hey Miss, when are we going for that drink?" Education orderlies with their red t-shirts, with EDUCATION SUPPORT printed proudly on their backs, were ushering wayward students towards the gates.

She climbed the stairs towards the Education Department and unlocked the gates. Here there was a brightness and energy. Prisoners' paintings lined the walls. There was a board displaying poetry and creative writing. Another board showed posters, which told of coming events, courses, helplines, and the Equal Opportunity, Race Relations and Anti-Bullying mission statements. She turned into the tiny staffroom/office and greeted the other teachers, who were busy preparing their classes, photocopying, looking through books, collecting their registers.

"Good morning, Tuesday gang", she called to the other teachers. She left her things in a locked drawer, picked up her keys and walked up the corridor to her classroom. It was going to be a good day. She had planned an exciting lesson, trying to enliven a somewhat boring subject – Cashflow Forecast in Starting your own Business. The classroom was sunny. Four big windows with bars, overlooked the exercise yard, and the workshops opposite. She had put up some lively posters displaying her subject. She had put pretty plants on the window sill, and generally the classroom was welcoming and, apart from the bars, could have been anywhere in a college.

She wrote the objective of today's lesson on the whiteboard under the date: CASHFLOW FORECAST …By the end of this session, you will know how to prepare a Cashflow Forecast, you will know why a Cashflow forecast is important, you will know the basics of a spreadsheet, you will know how to write simple formulae... She unlocked her cupboard, and put out her reference books, and worksheets, unlocked the computers, filled in the "tools are correct" form, and waited for her class. Her register showed that she had sixteen students, and hopefully some or most would arrive.

She hoped the new ones would settle and not be a problem.

They came in ones and twos, gossiping noisily, sliding into the chairs, greeting her and each other cheerfully. There were two new guys, both slightly overwhelmed by the class, who sat quietly in the corner of the room waiting apprehensively to see what they would be asked to do.

She called the class to order, and gradually they settled. Twelve. Big class. The room looked strangely too small for these big men, with big personalities. She greeted the two new men with a beaming smile. She knew how difficult it must be for them to come into this noisy, cheerful, unfamiliar environment. She was always aware that most of these students had had bad experiences of education, had probably caused many headaches for their teachers in the past. Had almost certainly been expelled, suspended, and the two new students were probably expecting some humiliation for their lack of schooling and knowledge. They were not going to be humiliated in her class.

Beaming brightly, she welcomed them and asked for their first names, introduced the other students, and asked for the Education Supports to move next to them. She assured them that, as soon as the others were given some work, she would come to see them personally and chat about their aspirations for starting a business.

She gave the class a puzzle as an ice breaker: Adam, the bright one, with sharp intelligent eyes and a ready smile, quickly settled to work it out. Den, quiet and shy, with little self confidence, was asking him for some help. The two Education Supports, John and Bradley, were smiling encouragingly too and helping the new students with the puzzle. Everton, helpful Everton, the gentle giant, was asking if she wanted him to help her to give out the worksheets. Tall, lanky Elvis, brilliant at Maths, was going to be needed today, to help with applying some of the "workings" of his Maths expertise to an Excel spreadsheet. Marlon, the fidget, possible ADHD, was already groaning that he could not work out the puzzle, and that it was too hard, and that he would need to go to the toilet soon. The class was telling him to "shut up" and get on with it. The two "twins" Simon and Ainsley, not really "twins", but always together, were trying to compete with each other to solve the puzzle first. Mac was a "loner", did not like working with the others, was concentrating hard, with his pen in his mouth, mouthing the clues, and occasionally writing something quickly on his paper. Kev, the youngster, with his sweet smile, looked bewildered, and was gazing at her pleadingly – no, she wouldn't help him. He always got away with murder. David, the "joker", was, as usual, pretending to rip out his hair in the anguish of trying to work out the puzzle. And finally, the two new men, Edward and Phillip.

Prison....

A prison classroom...

A prison teacher......

Mistakes

"Into the Valley of Death," read Kate....

She was reading Tennyson's poem, to illustrate mistakes. The objective of the lesson was to show that we all make mistakes; that we have to live with the consequences; that the only way to live with those consequences was to learn, learn, learn. The *only* way we learn....and never make the same mistakes again. She was starting by looking at some of the great blunders of history:

Someone had blunder'd
Theirs not to make reply
Theirs not to reason why
Theirs but to do and die
Into the valley of death
Rode the six hundred.

"They were a bit stupid, Miss, don't you think?" It was a general response from the class.

"They didn't question the order, and the order was a mistake. So, six hundred of them rode against the Russian artillery and most died. Stupid, yes, but a mistake...? Someone made a mistake here, but should they have followed the order? Blindly? What was their reason for following this order?" She wanted them to distinguish the reasons for mistakes...she was guiding them to the "right" answers...

"I think they must have been a bit stupid though, really Miss," said Vince, "I mean the bloke who made the mistake, I mean that was terrible, but they shouldn't have followed the order."

"Do you all think that? Who made the biggest mistake? They did, for following an order which was clearly wrong, or the bloke who gave the order? They felt that to live with what they considered cowardice would be more difficult than to die..."

"Them, because it was a mistake to waste their lives, wasn't it?" argued Vince. "Anyone could have got an order wrong."

"Yes, but they thought it was somehow honourable to carry out the order. Maybe it was stupid? What do the rest of you think...? Yes, so you agree, they were stupid? No one thinks they were honourable? OK....Not honourable then..."

She continued reading from passages illustrating other "mistakes".

"In the Warsaw Ghetto, the Jews finally rose against the Nazis, but all died in the attempt. They knew they would. Was that a mistake, or was that a way of holding on to some of their dignity and giving their life for that dignity? The world thought that theirs was a waste of life, but again, guys, they would have lived with the knowledge that they hadn't even tried..."

"No, Miss, that was really brave," said Andy. "I really admire them for that sort of bravery. They weren't going to just lie down and take it. That's different from those people in the Light Brigade."

"Yep," the class agreed. "That wasn't a mistake. That was something else. Well brave."

"So, are you saying that some mistakes, or what people call mistakes are worthwhile and that sometimes people have values which override everything?" she prodded, "What about, when a child runs into the street and its mother smacks it out of fear for its life, has the child made a mistake? Has the mother made a mistake? So, actually what some call mistakes, others call bravery, stupidity, life....What do we do when we make mistakes? What can we do when we make mistakes? And is it important *always* to remain true to your values? After all, you have to live with your decision...for the rest of your life, guys..." Maybe she was being a little too obvious...?

There followed a general discussion about how it is good to learn from mistakes, and how we learn best from those mistakes. They were saying the right things, so far...She was definitely being too obvious.

"So, let's see now, do you think anything was learnt from the 'Charge of the Light Brigade'?"

"Yes," they agreed, "Ask someone if the order sounds stupid, and don't follow a stupid order."

"I bet the bloke who got the order muddled never made that mistake again," said Gary.

"Yes. Do you think we never make the same mistakes twice?" asked Kate. "And if those mistakes have dire consequences, like ending up in prison, as it is for all of you, do you learn from them?" She had put in the knife...and now what was going to happen?

"Well, I've got to live with my mistake," said Simon.

"Yep, I suppose we all have, "said John. "No one can live without making mistakes, Miss. You got to admit, and so we all end up living with the consequences."

"Absolutely," replied Kate. "Of course we can't go through life without making mistakes. Some are small, some involve killing nearly six hundred people, and we have to live with the consequences, but we learn from those mistakes…" The lesson was going pretty well, but her prodding continued.

"I made a stupid mistake, and that's why I'm here," said Simon.

"Well, I suppose, it is always mistakes that get you all in here," said Kate, beaming at Simon; he was making it easier for her to get to the point of her lesson.

"Yes, but my mistake was very stupid," Simon continued. "If you don't laugh… Don't laugh anyone….I'll tell you what happened."

"Yes. Go on," encouraged Kate. "We won't laugh."

She wondered as always what was coming and held her breath.

"Well you see, me and my co-d (co-defendant) we were walking down this High Street, when we see a jewellers. See, there was a woman putting out some jewels like, in the window of this jewellers."

"Don't tell us, you threw a brick through the window," somebody called out.

"No,worse. We had a think and we decided to rob it, like go inside and rob it. It looked easy."

Despite herself, Kate was drawn into the story.

"So, we thought, we'd better go and buy some stockings to put on our heads before going in to rob this jewellers. So we walked about a bit, and saw a newsagents. We went in and asked for stockings. They only had tights so we bought two pairs of black tights. We got the tights out of the wrapping and had them ready to put on our heads when we rushed into the jewellers."

Pregnant pause. What was coming next, thought Kate?

"So we run into this jewellers, pull the tights over our heads, and they're big thick ones, and we can't see a thing. We didn't know we'd bought the wrong tights."

The class burst out laughing.

"You said you wouldn't laugh, hey. The woman at the jewellers pressed the buzzer for the police, and we were falling over cos we couldn't see anything. That was a mistake, Miss, a big mistake…"

Kate was trying not to laugh. Oh dear, the point of the lesson was somehow unravelling….

"Yes, but in a way, you can't call that a mistake, because it worked out right in the end," she said desperately. "You were thwarted in your robbery. Quite right too."

"Oh, Miss, that's not fair. If we'd got the proper tights it would have gone perfectly, see."

Something had gone badly wrong. Had anything that she had been saying gone in at all?

"Well, ours was an even bigger mistake," this time Malcolm.

"Oh no," said Kate, "please don't tell me that you tried to rob someone and you hit a problem…"

"Well, yes Miss. We had these guns and we were trying to rob a sub-post office. We'd gone in shouting and shouting, get down, over by the till, all of you… over by the till. We were sort of waving the guns around to scare people, and they were going to lie down by the till like we told them."

"Oh my God," breathed Kate, "how dreadful for those people. How could you?"

"No, Miss, wait, Miss, we were really kind in the end. See this post office had a bit that was a grocery bit, and there was this old lady and she was standing round by the grocery bit, and we didn't see her at first. When I see her, I said to her, look love, you got to go and lie down with the others. And I waved my gun around a bit."

"God, you could have killed someone," said Kate.

"No, Miss, we weren't actually going to kill anyone, we were just frightening them."

"Oh that's alright then," said Kate. The irony was lost.

"So, we're trying to get this old dear to go round by the till to lie down with the others, and she says, no I can't do that, cos my daughter-in-law waits at home for me, and if I don't come home in half an hour, she calls the police to go and find me.....Fantastic. Brilliant....So I say to her again, no..... you got to go and lie down by the till, and she says no.... because my daughter-in-law will call the police. So we get into this argument..... I'm telling her to lie down by the till, and she's telling me that she can't...... I wave my gun around a bit more, but it's no use. She won't go and lie down. Well what could I do?"

"Oh my God," whispers Kate, "what did you do?"

"Well, I'm not a murderer, am I, Miss? I'm a nice guy. So I say to her in the end, well, you'd better go to your daughter-in-law and.....I say to the others, you'd better get up and go home and then.... we all scarper."

"Oh my God," repeats Kate. "But you scared all those people, traumatised them, how could you?"

"Oh Miss, I thought you would be proud of the way I was kind to that old dear. I could have made her go and lie down, and I didn't."

"Yes, but not because you were kind, but because you had no other way out," Kate insisted.

"No, that's true, but really I wouldn't have harmed any of them, really, Miss, you know I wouldn't."

"They didn't know that. God give me strength. I give up."

"You got to admit, Miss," said someone else, "they didn't hurt anyone."

Were she and they living on different planets? Could values be so skewed? Should she give up now?

She felt utterly helpless, but how could you change those values? How could she get them to hear her? Was it impossible?

Would they ever hear her?

Milgram's experiment

Kate didn't mind teaching the VPs (Vulnerable Prisoners, who choose to be segregated for their own protection, often sex offenders). Some teachers found it difficult. She felt ambivalent, who wouldn't? She abhorred their crimes but they were human beings, and she felt that, professionally, she had to teach them. She was a prison teacher, and so had no option as to whom she would teach. Whenever anyone from "outside" challenged her about her feelings for these "animals", she found it difficult to explain herself. At first, she tried: because they are human beings, you could like them; you could never forgive them, that was for their victims to do; yes, she could identify with the victims but she could show them, the perpetrators, human feelings, because she was human; because as you got to know them, it was easy to treat them with respect and dignity, because she was not like them.

It sounded as if she knew the answer, but basically, she had never really analysed what she felt in the VP Unit, and if she tried, she found that she was unable to explain totally. Feelings were not rational. It became so difficult to explain, that gradually, she began to avoid conversations about her students, and if anyone from the outside asked what she did, she told them she taught adults, without specifying who those adults were. If anyone challenged her more, she found herself defending people who she knew she was really unable to defend. Their crimes were indefensible, that was true, but people did not, could not, understand why she could talk and laugh and relate to people who were so "bad". And neither could she, really. And the more she defended, the more she sounded like some "do-gooder", which she wasn't. It was her job, finally, and she would do it to the best of her ability.

One of her students had been convicted of sexual assault. He was a small, insignificant man, with a face which resembled an unattractive horse, long, too long for the rest of his body, baleful, acne-scarred. His redeeming feature was his eyes, which were somehow composed at all times. This may have indicated apathy, resentment, lack of emotion, who knows what. But his eyes were his one attractive feature. Bright blue, intelligent, sad. When he came new to her class, she asked, as she always did, how was his victim, and he had replied that she was fine, OK, nothing to worry about.

Then one day, he burst out with the story and cried inconsolably. Were they crocodile tears, she wondered, but was moved. He hurt, and she was sensitive to any human being who hurt. He told everyone how unattractive he felt, how he envied his friends who could pick up girls, just like that. He hadn't even tried to ask a girl out, and he was 21. One day a beautiful girl came into his shop, and flirted with him. She laughed, as no one had laughed with him before. Her head thrown back, she joked with him and laughed. She was dressed prettily, had on a low-cut blouse, a pair of jeans, and she laughed so much. When she left the shop, he followed her, dragged her into an alley-way and made her kneel before him, and perform oral sex. She wasn't laughing at him then.

Kate felt the revulsion in her throat. She felt overwhelming sorrow for the poor victim. The girl had only laughed, and was punished so dreadfully. How was she now? Probably traumatised beyond belief. What is more, how would she, Kate, feel if she heard that some wretched prison teacher was now talking to the man who had wrecked her life, as if…

"How could you do that?" she challenged him. "Why did you think you had the right to humiliate another person in this way?"

"She humiliated me, Miss. Don't feel sorry for her. She was a bitch."

Kate tried not to show the anger that almost made her hit him.

"Don't you dare call another woman a bitch in this classroom. Please just tell us all, why a woman who laughs with you is a bitch?"

"Because she laughed cos I am ugly and she is beautiful."

"How could you possibly know that? How could you possibly tell why she was laughing?"

"I know. I knew".

"You don't know. You don't *know* that. You didn't know her. She was an innocent girl who laughed with you. How could you have judged her before knowing her?"

Kate decided to leave the subject, as she was letting her emotions dictate her actions, and she might well hit him straight in his god-damned stupid eyes. She couldn't resist one last comment:

"I suppose you are the lord of the universe, and everyone who comes in contact with you focuses only on you. They don't have a life, and all they can think of, is how to laugh at you. Hah!! Mr. Goddamn, f…. Universe. Well, let's leave it like that."

But she felt sorry for him as well, because he had absolutely nothing – nothing to be proud of, nothing to boast to his friends about, no personality, no outer beauty, no inner beauty. He was just empty, like a dirty, crystal vase, which had once been beautiful but in which the flowers had died long ago, and had not been washed. The smell of the dead flowers still pervaded the senses, and the vase was stained and dirty. She could never justify what he had done, and that night she could not sleep for the thoughts that lingered in her mind – the innocent girl, the poor, innocent girl. Kate was unable to get the victim out of her head. How she must have felt, that dreadful evening. How she probably felt now. The dirty vase had contaminated the poor girl with its smell, and its dirty flowers and its stains. Kate wept for the girl, but she had to help the perpetrator, that was her job. Her job was to protect every other innocent girl who came into contact with him.

She had been given the job of teaching "Health" to the VPs. At first she had declined, as she had no idea what to teach them, and "Health" was not a subject she would enjoy. She had trained as a Counsellor – but she was a teacher first, and she had no intention of counselling anyone in the prison. She knew that to counsel inside, she would need extra skills, and she was not remotely interested in counselling here. However, she was committed to Public Protection, and to improving the well-being of her students. She took the job in the prison, not to change the world, but to do something to improve it, however small.

The next session, she had prepared her lesson on Perception.

In the VP Unit, she had a tiny classroom, which regularly overflowed. Her students were squashed in like proverbial sardines, but she took as many as she could. Today 15 of them sat to learn about "Health". She saw that Henry, the sexual assaulter (how could she label him?) was sitting in the corner, with his doleful, unhappy expression.

On the board, she had written, PERCEPTION. By the end of this lesson, you will know what we mean by perception and how our perception of what is happening is not necessarily everyone's perception.

She stood in front of the class, and let the noise quieten down. She stood an extra fifteen seconds in silence.

"I'm going to tell you a story," she said. "It is just a story that I made up, so it's not the truth. Yesterday, a woman came to see me at home. I don't know this woman very well, but I've seen her around. She knocked on my door and started crying. I asked her in, and she poured out her woes. For three hours she poured out her woes. Three unhappy hours, because she was a very unhappy woman, and her tears punctuated her story. My God, she had problems.

Today, I went to the supermarket. In the distance I saw this woman. I smiled at her. I looked sympathetically at her. I knew she had problems. And....she ignored me. She glanced at me and she ignored me. She actually scuttled down a neighbouring aisle not to meet with me. Yesterday, I spent three hours listening to her. Listening to her goddamn problems, when I had work to do, and today she was ignoring me."

The class sat in silence. You could hear a pin drop. Even "doleful faced" Henry looked interested.

"Why the hell was she ignoring me? How could she do that? She should be grateful. She should be pleased to see me.

OK, all of you. Why *was* she ignoring me? Peter....?"

She wrote down their answers on the whiteboard.

"OK, Peter thinks she was embarrassed, because she had told me too many personal things....Good point, Peter. James...?"

"She didn't see me...yes, but I was quite close...oh right, she was too troubled to see me, she was focused on her problems. Good point, James."

After a few minutes, she had all their ideas on the whiteboard. She was a bitch, who wasn't grateful. She was an ignorant cow, who couldn't say thank you. There were many reasons why she hadn't spoken to Kate.

Kate stopped dramatically again. Allowed a few seconds to go by, and turned to them again.

"Which of those reasons was the correct one? Why had she ignored me? Who thinks she hadn't seen me..? Quite a few of you. Who thinks she is just an ignorant cow who has no manners? Hmmm, you're not sure...

How am I going to feel... *feel*, guys, towards her if I think she is an ungrateful cow? Yes, I'm going to be very angry. How dare she? How dare she ignore me after keeping me listening to her all afternoon? What might I say to her? Yes, not nice...I'm going to attack her with a lot of verbals. Who the hell does she think she is? How can she use me, like this? How dare she? How dare she?

Hey guys, but what if she really didn't see me? How will *she* feel when she gets this stuff thrown at her? Yes, but she deserves all I give her. Doesn't she? I'm the one who decides, aren't I? Who decides, guys? Does she decide? Ultimately, how will I know why she ignored me?"

The answer is always so obvious that Kate wonders why they never "perceive" it at the beginning of her lesson. She had even tried this exercise with her colleagues, and their answers were the same as her students' answers.

"So, I need to ask her. I need to go up to her, and ask her. Not in a hostile, angry, abusive manner, but politely, pleasantly, respectfully. And here is where we get to it...we do this all the time. Not just you. I do it too. We think we can guess, even know what other people are thinking, because we, the gods of the universe, have the power of complete knowledge. What is more, we all have the same perception of events, don't we?"

Kate had reached them. They were interested. Leonard spoke up...clearly we were not so well endowed with knowledge and we certainly did not have the same perception of events as other people, in fact…and he launched into his own story, about how he had thought he had seen something, but in fact.. (oh, what a clever dick he was…) The class began to discuss how tricky it was not to jump to conclusions. And how dangerous.

"And I have another one for you," interrupted Kate finally.

"We write scripts. We write scripts that other people are *supposed* to read and learn and then talk to with us. I have had a wretched day at work. Nothing has gone right. But all is well. My husband, a good man, will greet me when I come home from work. He will immediately see that I have had a wretched day, won't he? He will welcome me into the house as I walk to the front door, with a glass of wine and slippers ready in his hand. He will help me to a comfortable armchair. He will sit in the other chair and listen to all my problems, won't he? Anyway, he has the script. I hope he has learnt the words. What do you think happens when I get home?"

They are laughing. Of course, he hasn't learnt the script. Of course, he doesn't have the wine and the slippers and the comfortable armchair ready.

"What's more, he doesn't want to listen to my problems." Kate says with a flourish. "In fact, he wants to tell me about his. How insensitive. How lacking in understanding. Typical man! What the hell is he thinking of? He has not learnt his script. He doesn't even know that there is a script. What is wrong with him? I would have known. I would have cared for him. I am the saint." Her face crumples into her self-righteous expression and the class laughs a little more.

Henry is not laughing. In fact, he has started to cry. Oh bugger, she's upset a student. He begins to sob, as the class starts to look embarrassed and silence falls again.

She walks over to Henry and puts her arm round him.

"What's happened? What is it Henry? What did I say? Was the class that bad?"

He continues to cry and she looks with mock astonishment at the rest of them.

"What did I do?" Immediately she feels ashamed. No one is mocked in her class, she always maintains, and yet she's mocking him now. She turns to him with genuine interest.

"Henry, what did I say? How have I upset you?"

"It's the girl. You see, she wasn't laughing at me. I just used it as an excuse, didn't I? Just an excuse to rape her. That's what you're saying, aren't you? You're right. You're right. It was just an excuse."

"Class, that's not what I've been saying, is it? I didn't say that we used our lack of perception as an excuse to bully, humiliate, or harm another human being. We may do, and that's another matter. But mostly, we think that our perception is right, because we haven't asked the other person for their perception. Isn't that what I've been trying to teach this morning?"

Henry continued to cry. Eventually, when the class had finished, he came up to Kate and asked her if he should write to his victim and apologise. How could he make it up to her? What could he say? She must think that he is absolute filth. She must hate him more than she has hated anyone. What does he do now?

Kate didn't know.

"You can't do anything, Henry, you can't do anything now. I don't know what will help, but you can make it up in some other way. Try to think overnight what you can do to make it up. But you can't write to her. A no-no, Henry, you know that."

How could she not feel sorry for him now? When the truth had been revealed to him, what does he do with this truth?

He became her best student. He was always by her side, politely helping, and eventually organising a self-help group inside, which did not pull punches, and challenged others who might justify their crimes.

Then came that fateful lesson. She had been talking of Milgram's experiments.

She had written the objective on the whiteboard, "By the end of this lesson, you will know how easy it is to be influenced by others. What is more, you will know how easy it is to be influenced by others with authority."

"Right guys," she started, "How many of you are influenced or think that you may be influenced by what other people say?"

A few hands went up.

"Hey, the truth. Let me tell you. What our parents taught us influences us more than you will know. It is as if we have this inner message, parent-speak within us. They may not have deliberately taught us things, but we have internalised them nevertheless.

My mother, an elegant, fashionable woman, yes...I haven't taken after her, thank you....who was more than obsessed with what the world thought about her and particularly how she looked. Unbelievable, you may say. What does it really matter what the world thinks? Does the world think about us anyway, or does the world think about its own problems, and has no time for ours?"

Geoffrey, a student who had started the class a week ago, sat quietly at the front of the class. He was a person whose emotions seemed to swing hither and thither, like a massive pendulum. One day, he would be sitting very quietly, totally absorbed in the class, the next day, he would be chatty and interrupting. Today, thanks be to God, he was having one of his quiet days...may it continue, she thought.

"Well, of course, I was not going to be like my mother. I despised her absorption in how people were dressed, why people were dressed as they were, why they weren't dressed like her, or at least why they weren't dressed in what she thought was appropriate. Absolutely despised it. Then, one day, I went to a First Holy Communion Mass – I'm a catholic – there was a group of girls sitting towards the back of the church. And one of them had a backless dress on. A backless dress? God almighty, didn't she know that you didn't wear backless dresses in church? Who the hell had advised her to wear a backless dress? How demeaning. How lacking in respect.

Guys, that was me...that was me, judging a young girl by what she was wearing. Who had taught me that backless dresses were a no-no in church? My mother! Who thought she knew what was the right thing to wear in church? My mother! Who thought she knew what God told us to wear in church? My mother? But my mother wasn't there. I was. Aaaagh," Kate pretended to keel over, "I was becoming my mother. Not her good values, but this stupid value of judging people by what they wear, and what they should wear."

The class was laughing. Geoffrey did not laugh, but sat quietly, absorbed in his thoughts.

"You OK, Geoff?" she asked.

"Yes, Miss. OK."

"Do you think that certain nations are more judgemental than others?" she got their interest again. "Are the British judgemental? Who's British here? Are we judgemental? Of course not. We are the example of non-judgementalism. Are the Germans? They judged the weak, the crippled and the Jews. So, they must be judgemental. Or are they just good at following orders?

Milgram?....Milgram, a US psychologist thought that the Germans, based on the experience of the Second World War, were judgemental, and that they followed rules and authority without question. Anyway, he decided to do some experiments on the Germans to see why they obeyed orders without question. In order to prepare, he decided to try the experiment on some American students at Yale University. Now, these students were intelligent, bolshy and American. They did not follow orders easily. The experiment was going to involve an actor, who would appear to be one of the students but "randomly", (Milgram arranged this), chosen to be the "victim". The students were told that they would be taking part in an experiment which would help the "victim's" memory. They would be asked to ply him with questions, and if he answered the questions wrongly, he would be given an electric shock. This electric shock would be increased until the final one would be so dangerous, it would be life threatening. The actor sat behind a glass screen, and pretended to be in agony as the electric shocks increased. He begged the students not to continue. Sitting beside the student taking part was a man in a white coat, and when each student tried to complain, or desist from applying the electric shock, the man in the white coat, told them to continue, that it was necessary to continue, that the experiment required them to continue. Most of them continued, guys. They were deeply upset, and some were crying, but they continued, because the man in the white coat, the authority figure, asked them to do it. Bolshy, intelligent, Americans continued to inflict pain on another human being because they had been told by an authority figure that they must, that it was necessary."

Kate stopped. She was a good teacher. They were affected. Again, you could hear a pin drop.

"Would I have continued? Who knows? Would you have continued? Who knows? Who knows what we are capable of doing when an authority figure tells us to do it? The Germans? Hmmmm? Milgram realised that it had nothing to do with being a German, we are all capable...."

The class, after the initial horror, started to discuss the experiment. How many had desisted? How had it affected them to know what they were capable of? Some had nervous breakdowns. God. We humans, are we complicated?

Kate finished the lesson. Geoffrey was still very quiet, and quietly left with the other somewhat subdued students.

Kate went back to the Education Department.

During the afternoon, her Manager called her into the office. Geoffrey had attempted to commit suicide at lunchtime, and had been taken to an outside hospital in a coma. Kate couldn't believe what she heard. She told her Manager that he had been subdued at the end of the lesson, and that the lesson was a tricky one, but he was fine when he left. She found it difficult to concentrate on her class during the rest of the day. The prison, as was usual after a suicide attempt, was very affected. Prison officers were going round their duties very quietly. There was general sympathy for the victim and for the officer who had found him. Apparently, he had been taking some medication, which he had pretended to swallow, as he picked it up every morning and afternoon, but somehow had saved it and took all the pills at once, and lost consciousness. His cell mate called an officer, who tried to save him, and managed to make him vomit up some of the tablets, but some of them must have had an impact and he had not regained consciousness when the ambulance arrived.

The next morning there was a meeting in the chapel, and the Governor told them that Geoffrey was still very sick and still in a coma.

Kate was beside herself. Was it something she had said? Or done?

Her Manager called her into the office again during the morning, asked her about the lesson yesterday, which Kate repeated to her, and then told her not to blame herself, not to worry but to go home and rest.

That evening, her Manager phoned her to say that Geoffrey had not regained consciousness yet, but that unfortunately, the Governor was unhappy with her lesson, that he was suspending her, pending enquiries, and that she was not to return to work until further notice. Her Manager asked if she could do anything for Kate, maybe she could meet with her tomorrow, and chat to her, and that she wasn't to worry, everything would sort itself out.

Kate was devastated. She felt sick and restless. She managed to get through the evening with help from a bottle of wine, and finally fell asleep in an armchair, then tossed and turned all night and woke in the morning feeling frightened and full of despair.

What had she said, in her class? What the hell had made Geoffrey take his own life? Christ, was she to blame? She would not do that ruddy lesson again. Self-doubts and guilt assailed her like a proverbial ton of bricks all the next day. She couldn't eat a thing. Her husband told her that she was not doing herself a favour by not eating, and drinking too much wine. So she told him to F... Off, and mind his own business, and thanked him profusely and ironically for being helpful.

She didn't know how she got through that week. She tried to read, but couldn't concentrate. She tried to watch DVDs but found she was getting too emotional at the least emotion and bursting into tears. She slept because she was tired during the day, which meant that she couldn't sleep at night, and her fears multiplied a thousand-fold in the dark and she felt lonely and sad and frightened. She was frightened that she could cause someone so much anguish that they had tried to kill themselves. She was distraught that she had not reported that Geoffrey was acting unusually. But the truth was, he was not acting unusually. He always had these mood swings. She kept going over the lesson, over and over. She blamed the prison. If Geoffrey had been suicidal, then the officers who were with him all day should have spotted something. How could she be to blame when she only saw him for a couple of hours or so? Then she would blame herself, for a lack of insight, and a stupid lesson. But then she had done that lesson hundreds of times, and so it was the prison that was at fault. Why had the psychiatrists allowed a susceptible bloke in her class? But then had he been quieter than usual that day? If only she had...if only...

On the following Monday, she was asked to come for an interview with one of the Governors. She could ask a union representative or a friend to be with her, but she refused either. He told her that he was going to ask her some questions about the counselling she did in her classroom. She didn't do counselling, she was teaching Health, and more recently Lifeskills. He informed her that one of the officers had been told by one of the students that she had been counselling. This was absolutely untrue. She taught Lifeskills, she didn't counsel. Which one of the officers had said that that was the case? And which one of the students? The Governor was very polite and pleasant, but he was clearly, to her at least, unequivocal in his judgement of her. He asked her how she would describe counselling? It's when the counsellor and client work together towards a solution. He asked her how different would she suggest was her class? She told him that her class was a class, she was teaching people ways of coping. He smiled and asked her how was that different than working with them to learn to cope as in counselling. She told him that she felt that she was being made a scapegoat because of a suicide attempt, which had not been her fault. He assured her most politely that that was not the case, and that he was merely trying to get at the truth. He asked her to repeat her lesson to him. That lesson sounded fateful when she repeated it, even she had self-doubts about it, so why shouldn't he doubt her? She knew really that she had more or less sealed her fate that day.

Three weeks later, her Manager asked to meet her for a coffee in a café nearby. Kate could come back to work from the following Monday, but she was not to do any more "counselling". Her manager thought it wise for Kate not to carry on with the Lifeskills classes in the VPU (Vulnerable Prisoners' Unit), and would instead, start working with the drug rehabilitation unit.

"I'm sorry Kate, it's not that I don't trust you, it's just that if there is another misunderstanding in the prison, and you lose your job…. I think we'll play it safely, at least for a while."

Kate had to agree.

Six weeks after that, Geoffrey came out of hospital. He had come out of the coma, and was transferred back to the prison.

Kate went to see him.

"Hey, Geoff, how are you? What happened?"

"I don't know Miss. I just couldn't go on like that… Sometimes, I just couldn't go on, so I decided to top myself, cos it would be better if I was dead, wouldn't it? Sometimes the sadness was too much, see…"

"Yes, Geoff, I see…"

"You not teaching us no more, Miss. I like your lessons. Best thing in the week. Had a laugh. Hmmmm. Come and teach us again, please."

"I can't, Geoff. I'm not allowed to any more.."

"Yeahhhh, best thing in the week. Made me feel better, really interesting some of that stuff. Only thing that made me feel better. Please, Miss…"

"Can't Geoff…"

She walked away from the unit. She walked away from Geoff.

The Ghost

"So, how are you going to move your tools, Ricky?"

Kate was working with her "special" (special needs), who was already helping with the gardening in the local hospital, and wanted to start his own business, doing some gardening privately.

"Class, guys, can you stop what you're doing and help Ricky here. As you know, he wants to be a gardener for people, to help older people, and he doesn't drive, so we have a problem here because he has to move his tools somehow."

"Shanks's pony, Ricko." James was being so helpful today.

"Miss?" Ricky was confused.

"Walking Ricky, walking."

"Don't be silly, James, that's stupid, he can't walk that far with a load of spades and stuff on his back." Pragmatic Fred. "He'll have to get the bus, and then what? He can't knock over the passengers."

"Probably kill them with his spades in the attempt," muttered James.

"Get a motorbike mate, and put the stuff in a little sidecar," suggested Tony.

"Tone, I don't think it would be a good idea for Ricky to get a motorbike, mate." Pragmatic Fred again.

Ricky was special, and Kate knew that really he was not going to be able to manage by himself on the outside, and that he was certainly not going to be able to run a business, but through this class she could teach him so much else, and the others too.

The trouble with Ricky was that he looked so innocent, a little black cherub, with mischievous, laughing eyes, sparkling teeth to match and a ready, full-on smile. You could not resist the charm, and everyone including her treated him a little like a child, and protected him.

However, she did not tolerate everything from him. Ricky's obsession was with hugging people, hugging them extremely tightly. Unfortunately, not everyone, in fact, extremely few people liked to be hugged by a total stranger, let alone, very tightly; and it got him into trouble inside and out. She had given him two golden rules:

"You must never, ever touch a woman. And you must never look longingly at her breasts. Inside or out."

"What's long..ing...ly, Miss?" he enquired mischievously.

She demonstrated a look of great longing, in fact great lechery; Casanova himself wouldn't have bettered the look.

"And what happens if you look longingly at a woman's breasts or hug her?"

"I get suspended for a week, Miss."

"In here, Ricky. And on the outside?"

"I get put in prison, Miss."

"So, we know where we stand."

She had had to have him suspended already, because he had hugged a new female teacher. Had really pushed his luck. The teacher was very new, and was probably going to end up in therapy for the rest of her life.

"Ricky," she said, "remind me, what happens if you hug a teacher?"

"You're not going to suspend me, Miss, please." Oh those eyes and that smile, he could put on the charm when he wanted to.

"No, I've warned you. You will be suspended for a week. No arguing."

"Yes, Miss."

The other students were very tolerant towards him. Unfortunately also for them, they had to be tolerant of his stifling hugs, which Ricky would be constantly subjecting them to, as he couldn't touch women. They never complained, though.

One day, he had come into the classroom very full of himself.

"See, Miss. About not touching a woman; what if I ask a woman to dance? I gotta touch her, don't I?"

"Hmmmmm. A woman is not as strong as a man, Ricky, so whatever you do, you've got to protect her. You must never frighten her. If you hug her like you do, she gets frightened. She thinks you're going to harm her."

"But I ain't. Why would I?"

"She doesn't know that, does she? Or do you have a big sign round your neck which says I only want to hug you tightly, and look longingly at your breasts, but I don't want to hurt you. Men can't do that or women get frightened."

"Nahhh, I don't have a sign, Miss."

"So, you've got to let her know in other ways. It's called body language."

"Body language, Miss?" He looked puzzled.

By now she felt like that young woman in Seven Brides for Seven Brothers, teaching her brothers-in-law how to treat women.

"Goin courtin' goin courtin', la la lalalalalala la laaaaa.

Oh it sets your senses in a whirl

Dudin' up to go and see your gal...La la la la

Goin' courtin'..."

On the board, she should have had the objective..."By the end of this lesson, you will know how to go courtin'..." Perfect for an inspection.

"Look," she demonstrated to Ricky, "how do I look now?"

"Dunno, Miss. Cross?"

"Yes, and now...?"

"Dunno, Miss, dunno, how do you look?"

"She looks happy," grumbled James. "Or slightly manic," he added muttering.

God, it was hard. Of course, Ricky could not read body language, nor expressions.

"What I'm trying to say.... James...?"

"Yes Miss, I think what she's trying to say, Ricko, is that it's not what you say, it's how you look that matters."

"Well, not quite...I think it's best if you don't dance with anyone ever. And don't touch them and NEVER look longingly at their breasts."

One day, Ricky had come in very frightened.

"Miss, I got a ghost in my cell."

"Oh my God, what sort of ghost?" queried Kate.

"I dunno, it makes a lot of noise in the night. And it moves my things in the day."

"Well, it can't be a ghost, Ricky. There are no such things as ghosts."

"Yes, there are Miss, I seen one," Lee put in his pennyworth.

"God, Lee, where did you see a ghost?" the class wanted to know.

"Well it was one day, I was walking…" and he launched into a long, horror saga embellished with many pregnant pauses and eye rolling…."so, there you are then, Miss, there are ghosts."

"Well, my grandmother used to say," Kate had got drawn into the story, "that if you see a ghost, you should say, Spirit, what can I do for you, because it's probably an unhappy ghost."

"See, Ricko," Lee said, "that's what you gotta do tonight, innit?"

"Well, yes," said Kate, "only there aren't such things as ghosts. My grandfather said, and he was a forester, that people "saw" ghosts all the time in the forest, but he was in the forest more than anyone else and he never saw a ghost."

"I saw a ghost once," said another of her students, "well I never actually see it, but I knew it was there, cos it was moving about a lot."

"Well," said Kate again, "it doesn't mean it was a ghost. My friend thought she saw a woman kneeling at her piano one day, and I told her that it was probably the shadow of the piano playing tricks on her. Shadows sometimes play tricks on us."

By now poor Ricky looked even more frightened than when he had first started.

"Miss, what am I gonna do then? Shall I ask it what it wants, like you said?"

"I didn't say that exactly, Ricky. Now, you haven't actually seen it, have you? Someone, an ordinary human being, could be making the noises, and moving your stuff around, couldn't they?"

"I don't think so Miss, why would they do that? And there are some real evil spirits in this place, aren't there? And someone told me that one of them who was hanged, used to be in my cell, see?"

The prison used to be a hanging prison, and the bodies were laid to "rest" or whatever, right by the walls, underneath a patch of lawn. People said that they were buried so shallowly that their bones stuck out every so often, but Kate who had been to check, naturally, had never seen any bones. In fact, she had never felt any evil or other spirits in prison. Probably with all the officers around, it was the safest place in the world.

Recently though, the old lift which used to bring food up from the basement in one of the wings, had started moving up and down of its own accord. Everything had been checked and there seemed nothing wrong with it. The chaplain was asked to exorcise it. He told Kate that he had felt a bit of a "plonker", because he was convinced that it was some mechanical fault which was causing all the "hoo-hah". He thought the prison authorities were similarly unconvinced about it being some spirit from the beyond, but to reassure the prisoners and staff, he had to exorcise the lift, which he did with great ceremony, and the lift stopped misbehaving.

Kate wondered if, whoever was playing tricks on poor Ricky, had got his idea from the lift fiasco.

"Listen, Ricky. I promise you it is not a real ghost. Promise." Kate assured him. "But what I will do is go and ask your wing officer to move you to a different cell. Will that help?"

"Ooh yes," replied Ricky. "I don't want to be in a cell where there was a man who was hanged."

Kate dutifully went to see the officer, who assured her that he would move Ricky immediately.

"No one who was to be hanged was ever kept in this wing," he said. "They're just scaring old Rick."

Next day, Kate wrote up her lesson on the board..."By the end of this lesson, you will know about the power of suggestion..."

Ricky never heard the ghost again.

The Competition

"In one word, good, good...as a simile....great, Malcolm, that's brilliant, a metaphor. Hard, isn't it...?"

Kate was doing creative writing in her Key Skills class. The class were competing with each other to describe their best day in various ways....

"What was it like, Andy, what was your best day like....a simile...like being in Heaven...wow. What's it like being in heaven, Andy, in one word....Nice...nice? It's seventy million times better than nice, come on...nice? Anyone, describe heaven..? Over the moon..? Very funny, Steve...

OK, here are some poetry books, find some words or phrases the poets use...ha haaaa...to describe something...um...nice. You particularly, Andy, with your nice...God, why do I bother? Nice...?"

The class were enjoying the lesson as usual. They loved the teasing, and the games. They knew how much she valued them and responded. One of them had told an inspector that her lessons were fun; then looked worried as though fun should not be used about a lesson. They said that her lessons made a difference to their dreary lives. They said that they had come to her lessons for "something to do", and then stayed. They said that when they had asked to do English, they thought it would be just a lesson, but these lessons were good. Kate made you feel like a poet, a presenter, a dramatist, a newsreader, a writer...Kate always made you feel good.

"Guys, an announcement. Listen to this:

The local library outside are running a competition, a poetry competition. Guess what...yes, the prison, you, my little poets are going to win this competition. We are going to show the world outside these walls what we're made of…Very funny, Steve...Puppy dogs' tails, very funny…I'm certainly not made of…I'm a woman…made of steel. I want you to start writing in your cells, from tonight. I want the best poetry ever to come out of your sweet pens, guys. We are going to win, and no, John, I'm not competitive, where on earth did you get that idea from?"

They wrote and they wrote. Poems came in like the proverbial waterfall. Every morning, the poems came in, and they just got better and better. Sometimes tears came to her eyes as she read them. She was so proud. Eventually, the final ten were chosen, and she sent them off.

Weeks later, so many weeks in fact that she thought that the poems had got lost in the post; that she had somehow forgotten to send them; that the library weren't interested; she got a letter informing her that four of the poems had been chosen. What is more, the poems were going up for an exhibition in the local library, and that the four poets were invited to come to the opening. Included, was a proper invitation: Drinks and nibbles, in the library to celebrate local poetry.

The class was ecstatic. Sadly, though, they would not be able to go to the opening. Or…Kate had an idea.

She wrote to the Governor, including the poems and the invitation. Could they not be granted a ROTL, a Release on Temporary Licence to go? Please.

She was backed by her Manager, who thought it was right and proper that the poets were there at their first exhibition. All four of them were not MAPPA'd (prisoners identified as a danger to Public Protection) and so were safe to go out of the prison and were not going to be any danger to the public. Please.

The Governor called the Manager and asked her advice.

He considered it.

They could go. Yessss. They could go, but on the proviso that they wouldn't drink any alcohol.

Kate wrote back to the Library informing them that she and the prison poets would be coming at 5 o'clock, and that would it be possible for the drinking not to start until they had gone at 7. From the invitation, she saw that the local MP would begin his speech at 7, so couldn't they do her an enormous favour and move the drinking till 7.

The Library agreed. They were very pleased that the prison would be sending the poets. In fact, they wrote to say that they would do anything to facilitate their coming.

That was all excellent.

Then Kate became nervous. Who would she take with her? Which member of staff? Two of them had to go with the four prisoners. She decided to take Luke. He was her colleague in the department and had contributed to the competition's success.

They were to go in two taxis, which would arrive and leave the prison at 4.45, and be back at 7.15. The prisoners would have to be back by 7.15, and she was responsible for their return.

That was not so rosy. What if they did a runner? What if they disappeared? The prison would go ballistic. She would never live it down. Whose idea was it to take four prisoners out? What on earth had possessed her?

"Now, if you, any of you, do a runner, I will chase you to the ends of the earth and kill you, slowly, I promise," she said to the guys. "The Governor is depending on me to bring you back and if you let me down…so help me, I will skin you alive." They were used to her over-the-top threats, and nothing would or could extinguish their excitement. They promised and promised that they would not let her down. But could she trust them? Really trust them?

As the days neared, she threatened them more and they promised and promised.

Finally, the day.

She and Luke were there at the gate. The taxi arrived. The four prisoners, in outside clothes (didn't they look different?), came out to the taxi. Last words from the officers. Last threats from her. Last half-hearted (how many times can you wholeheartedly promise?) promises from them.

So, it was she and Alan and Robert in one taxi, and Luke and Douglas and Chris in the other.

The taxis moved slowly out of the drive and began the journey down the High Road. It felt a little like a funeral cortege, the black taxis moving one after the other slowly down the High Road. Everyone in her taxi had by now quietened down, in fact, they all seemed to have been overcome by the moment. She felt worried, even anxious, but it could not quite subdue her pride and elation. This was a good moment. This made up for all the bad times in the prison. This made up for the low salaries, the cockroaches, the…the…Would she swap with anyone else at this moment? No, never. At this moment, there was nowhere else that she would rather be, and no one else…she was the proud prison teacher. She turned to look at Alan and Robert sitting on either side of her, and she gave them an encouraging look.

The taxis turned slowly to the right. There should be a prison officer walking in front, in place of the guy in the top hat, like in a funeral cortege, she giggled to herself.

The taxis negotiated the small road leading to the side of the Library. Slowly, slowly, they drew up to the entrance.

"OK, OK," she gabbled. "Here we are then. Hey, guys, good luck. So proud, so proud."

They bundled out of the taxis and stood for a moment in some disarray. Luke came up to her:

"You alright?" he said, "God, well done, Kate...well done."

Someone from the Library was there to usher them in, like royalty:

"You're from the prison. Yes, yes, this way...up the stairs...do you want to leave your coats? Here, you can leave them here. Well, well, from the prison? So pleased to see you all."

They walked into one of the rooms in the Library which had been transformed into a mini exhibition hall. Boards had been put up displaying the poems, which had been printed and enlarged. There were tables around the central table. People were already gathering, reading the poetry, talking and laughing to each other. On the central table were glasses, sandwiches, and... booze...alcohol! They'd forgotten to leave it till 7.

She looked at Luke searchingly. What the hell do we do now, her look was saying?

"Just one won't harm them," he said, "it's their day, Kate, go on..."

"But what if they don't stop at one, what if they get plastered, what if they run away...plastered...what will I say to the Governor?"

"They won't, Kate, they won't."

"OK guys," she gathered them round her. "It's like this, you're not supposed to have a drink, but, well, if I let you have one, will you promise to stop at one?"

Promise, promise, promise, promise. How many more promises could she want from them? And anyway did she really, really trust them to keep their promises?

"Go on then," she smiled at them. "I'm going to hang for this. They'll bring back the gallows just for me."

They took their glasses of white and red wine from the table and began to move around amongst the other guests. People surrounded them. "From the prison...? So you do poetry in the prison...? That's your teacher, but she's so petite..." Do they think we advertise for Russian women athletes for prison teachers, she thought. And did her students really need to look like cauliflower-eared, flat-nosed rugby players to match the perceptions of prisoners by the folk outside? She stopped herself getting annoyed. They were good people. They were trying to be friendly. Why was she getting so anxious? The wine...she thought. The wine...how many glasses would her lovely lot end up drinking? She could not look at anything. There was a knot in her stomach and she felt slightly sick. Hmmmm, so much for the proud, "petite" teacher.

Then Chris came up and asked her if she minded if he went to the toilet.

"Chris, you're on licence. You can go to the loo whenever you like." She spoke more confidently than she felt.

He went out. She went over to Luke.

"He's gone to the loo. What if..."

"Stop it Kate. So he's gone to the loo. Stop worrying. Enjoy," he said.

A group of people came in with children. They surrounded Douglas. He hugged them. Oh God, he's told his family to come. Now I won't be able to get him away from them at 7.

She went over to greet the family. "Yes, I'm his teacher. Oh he has, has he? I hope they were nice things. Never done this sort of thing before? Well, he's very talented. I bet you're proud." Proud? She thought, what a stupid word. She was up there with Andy for understating the obvious. She should go round and tell everyone how nice it all was, how very, very nice.

There was no sign of Chris.

Another group came in and ran up to Alan. Then more came in to be with Robert. She smiled and smiled:

"Did you all ask your families to come? How nice, how nice." She was never going to get them away at 7, and where was Chris?

By now she was feeling just ever so slightly hysterical.

More and more people were arriving and more and more of them were circling around the prisoners, who far from being overwhelmed, were being very natural and telling people about their poetry with enthusiasm and interest. She decided to go and look for Chris, and then he came in, also with his family.

"Chris, where have you been?" she asked him. "I've been so worried."

"Miss, I'm sorry. All the others had managed to get hold of their families, but I couldn't. So I've been trying to get hold of them this evening. Then I waited for them on the doorstep. They're here now."

"Oh, that's good, that's good," she muttered, slightly incoherent.

Chris joined the others. Everyone seemed to be having such a good time. Except her.

The minutes were ticking away. 6 o'clock, 6.30. Time was moving to 7. The local MP arrived. She recognised his face from the media. Her students were sticking to one glass of wine. How good were they?

At 6.55, she started rounding up the troops. "Sorry, guys, you have to say goodbye to your families now. Oh no, is your daughter crying, Robert? Oh I'm sorry, I'm sorry, we have to move. We have to move."

At 7, the chairperson quietened everyone down, and the MP moved towards the small lectern in the middle of the room.

"I'm so glad to be here," he said. "On my travels around the world..."

Suddenly a kerfuffle started. Quite a few people, namely prisoners and their families were making their way towards the exit. A child, Robert's daughter, was still crying bitterly.

"On my travels, around the world," repeated the MP. "I discovered that here in Britain..."

More kerfuffling, but no one, not one of the prisoners argued with her. As silently as they could, they made their way out of the library, and into the waiting taxis.

She wondered vaguely if the MP had felt that he had insulted someone by his speech...even before he had launched into it...had this group been offended by his travelling round the world and were they now protesting with their feet?...Oh well. The timing had not been great, but at least they were out.

Outside, she smiled at the families, and thanked them for their support. Last hugs, last goodbyes.

"Guys, thank you, thank you. You were brilliant. Why did I every doubt you?" she told them when they were settled.

"Miss, it's for us to thank you. Thank you for caring enough to give us an evening where we were tops and people talked to us, because we had done something good," said Robert.

Kate felt the tears as they trickled down her cheeks.

"Miss, Miss, what's the matter?"

"Nothing, absolutely nothing," she answered. The power of the understated.

The Escape

Kate had popped out for lunch. She was returning to the prison when she noticed some trouble in the drive. Police cars were everywhere with loud sirens blaring, the fire engine had arrived and then a couple of ambulances. People were gathered in the drive looking up at the roof of the main gate.

She could just distinguish a little figure prancing around on the roof, right up at the front of the gate. The figure seemed to be marching backwards and forwards, holding some sort of plackard.

The prison was "frozen". No one allowed in or out. After a while, she noticed that the Press had arrived. Quite a spectacle then.

She moved right up towards the gate, and saw that the figure was in fact, George, one of hers. What the hell..? His plackard, which was really just a piece of white paper from the Art Department, said:

"I want a propper dentist."

Propper, propper? How could he? His spelling had always been a problem. He was pacing up and down, enjoying the moment as far as she could see, and wanting a propper dentist. At times, he came right up to the edge, and the crowd uttered little shrieks of fear, anticipating seeing the little figure hurtling towards his demise. She would demise him, so help her, she thought...propper, how many times had she told him? And it would be on the news tonight.

George was one of her recidivists, back inside every now and then, always eager to come to Education, cheerfully greeting everyone with a "Well how's it all been then?" as if he he'd just popped out and was returning for a brief hullo, on his way to somewhere else. And then not doing anything for the few months he was inside, until he was out and the next time. He was always a cheerful soul and livened up the class with his little quips, and she wished he would liven up her life by doing some work, but no...every exercise, every assignment came back half done, or even not done, in fact, she thought she would have had an apoplectic fit from astonishment if he had completed his work. So maybe it was a good thing.

She wondered why he came to classes.

"Cos I want to learn Miss, I want to learn to write properly and read and all that..."

"But, George, you've got to work to improve yourself, it doesn't just happen from the sky. You're just using up precious space, and you know we have a waiting list...so, please..."

But no, George was full of promises, full of all the ambitious schemes and plans for when he did learn how to read and write properly, but never did anything about it.

One day, the Manager asked her if she could help clean up a new classroom they had been given in B Wing, to use for Induction. It was a long way from the Department and the classroom was filthy. Dog ends, (you aren't allowed to smoke in the prison), tea stains, bits of paper littered the whole room. She had asked George if he could come and help her. Whatever else, he was a cheerful companion and worked hard when asked to help practically.

When they saw it, both of them were somewhat dismayed. It looked like a big job. They decided to clean it up and then get some paint to give the walls a bit of a going-over.

They began by moving the furniture, piling it up at the back. Then they went in search of brooms, mops, cleaning rags and a floor polisher, together with cleaning stuff like polish and the prison equivalent of "Jif". As it was some way from the department, they decided to "borrow" the stuff they needed from the B Wing cleaners, so that they would not have to carry it all the way from the Education Department. Amazingly, George was a gem. He talked round the cleaners and the officers and eventually, even those women from that TV programme, "How Clean is your House?" would have been proud. They had managed to furnish themselves with everything that they would need to make this room a sight to behold.

Sweeping, mopping, washing…Kate complaining that she used to be a teacher…and now…finally, the room was ready for the polisher.

"George, you did say you know how to use this thing?"

"Course, Miss. It's easy. You got to mop really well, cos otherwise, you get a sort of wave-effect when the cleaner gets going. And all the dirt gets pushed around and around, like waves, see."

"Where do you put the polish?"

"Right there on the floor, Miss, see. You bung it on, the polish, and I just switch it on and it polishes."

Well, that's not quite what happened. Kate "bunged" on the polish. George switched on the cleaner and disappeared with it across the room, like a fairground waltzer. He clung to the handles and the cleaner waltzed off, with George clutching it for dear life. He managed to switch it off before too much harm was done.

"George, you don't know how to use it do you?" Kate cried, "You alright?"

"Yes, Miss. And no, I don't really know. But it looked easy when I see the cleaners doing it. Shall I have another go?"

He waltzed back to her. By then, both of them were in fits of laughter. Neither of them had any idea how to use the wretched thing, and as for any organised polishing, well....they would just have to polish where the polisher took George, and hope for the best.

"Look, let me have a go," said Kate after a while. "Give it here, maybe I can do a better job."

They switched it on, and this time Kate was waltzed across the room. The thing was a monster. It was so powerful. She tried to keep her feet on the ground, and had a horrible feeling that if she couldn't keep hold of it with her feet on the ground, the thing would waltz off, out of the room and down the wing, to goodness knows where, with her clinging on for dear life and her legs flying in the air behind.

George and she spent the rest of the afternoon, two hours, trying to work the polisher. They polished and polished, mostly over the same bit of flooring, and then would spend another ten minutes laughing and laughing. The room looked a picture. The centre gleamed, like an ice rink. The outside had what looked like skid marks all down it, and over by the chairs, the furniture....they had created waves of dirt, because they had not mopped very well in that area. A picture. Truly an NVQ pass in floor polishing.

The Education Manager came in to see how they were doing towards the end of the day. She looked very unimpressed (which was a surprise), and decided that she would also have a go at some polishing and also collapsed after a prolonged waltz down the ever more gleaming centre, into a chair, absolutely convulsed with laughter.

"If you just put the chairs over the bits of wave," she suggested, "no one will notice."

Unfortunately, when they moved the chairs, the chairs covered the sparkling bits of the floor, leaving the outsides with the waves, which made everything look worse. This meant that they had to have another go round the chairs and tables in the centre.

This sparked off another round of sweeping, mopping, "bunging" polish on the floor, and then being waltzed around like demented Mrs. Mops, and Kate fervently hoped that no one looked through the windows leading to the wing. She hoped especially that no one from the Ministry had been visiting, as after seeing what was going on in the Induction room, all observers would have to stay in a darkened room for a while, to recover.

Eventually, they thought they would have to leave it as it was. They could not better the effect.

And now here was George pacing around on the roof of the main gate, "protesting".

Three weeks later, he came back to the class.

"Hey, the protester," the class greeted him.

"...who can't spell proper," added Kate. "Hmmm?"

He laughed as usual, ever cheerful.

Later, he said he wanted a word with her.

"Miss, I wasn't actually protesting. I was escaping."

"Escaping?" Kate said, "Wow!"

"Yes, Miss, you can laugh, but I had come back from the dentist and then when they weren't looking I buzzed up the stairs, to escape."

"George, I have to admit, your escape plan was beyond reproach. I mean, escape…wow. You couldn't have planned it better. In front of the police, the fire engine, half the High Street, two ambulances and TV cameras…wow. An escape plan to beat all the escape plans, George."

"Yeah, well. I didn't expect the whole world and his missus to be there, did I?"

"So, they persuaded you to give up your escape plan in the end?"

"Yeah, it was the guys yelling from the prison, "Jump, jump," I thought I'd better give up… and I was hungry."

"Well, you can see their point of view," said Kate, "they were missing their visits and Education, and were locked in their cells for the afternoon. No wonder they were shouting for you to jump, heh?"

"I know, I shout as well when someone's on the roof, so I can't really say anything against them," answered George good-naturedly. "It's OK to protest and all that, but missing your visits…?"

"And now, spelling, you are never going to spell proper wrongly again, so help me!!" she laughed.

Thank you Father Christmas

Christmas morning.

As every Christmas morning, Kate came to the Prison chapel for the Christmas Mass. She loved this Mass, and always came to be here with the prisoners. It had become a tradition in her household that she would disappear early for the Mass, and return home for the present-opening and celebrations at lunchtime.

Everyone outside thought that she went to the Mass as some sort of saint dispensing her blessings to the prisoners on Christmas Day. Nothing could be further from the truth. She came because it was the only place for her to be on Christmas morning. She loved the atmosphere here. So, although much of the congregation had probably robbed people and murdered them, and came to the Mass just to get out of their cells, here she felt part of a close community, a community she understood and one she felt comfortable with. Comfortable? Because no one pretended, no one tried to be what they were not, and no one believed that he was holier than anyone else. Robbers, murderers, they may be, but certainly not hypocrites. Singing the carols, enjoying the prayers and the readings, Kate *enjoyed* the morning with them.

There were sad sights too, as when one year a young prisoner cried and cried like a child because he wanted his mother, and he couldn't get to see her; of course, it was Christmas Day and so no visits...but he still wanted his mother.

Kate arrived in the chapel. Normally a quiet, peaceful retreat, today it was abuzz with excitement. All the seats were taken, so Kate squeezed in along the side. The choir was sitting at the front, by the altar, over which hung an unusual cross made of railway sidings. When Judge Tumim was the Inspector of

Prisons, for his Desert Island Discs selection he wanted a disc of this choir singing. It was not so much for the quality of their singing, but for their enthusiasm and emotion. They could certainly sing heartily. Kate waved to them, and they gave her the thumbs up. Many of them were her students. All around people mouthed "Happy Christmas" at her and she mouthed back.

There were usually important visitors, sometimes the Mayor. In fact one year, some of Kate's students were sitting just behind the Mayor. The Mayor had on her chains of office, probably not gold, but very impressive. Kate's students winked at her and indicated that they would be having a go at the chains, fingers twitching near her back. Kate gave them a horrified look and they laughed. Of course it was just a joke, and they loved Kate to give them the "I am going to kill you any minute now, if you so much as think...think...of upsetting the mayor" look.

Her students loved Kate's threats. They were always so "over the top." However, sometimes...

One day, a class was misbehaving very noisily, and she was asked to come and intervene. She walked in and a hush fell in the room.

"Guys...outside, at the gates of Education, the undertakers are delivering coffins...yes, coffins, because if you don't stop this noise, I am going to kill you all and put you into those coffins...One nice thing is that if you stop immediately, I will let you...because I'm nice...I will let you... choose the hymns for your funeral. Fair, or not?"

Everyone laughed, except one poor soul put up his hand...

"Yes, David?"

"Miss, can I have "The Lord's my Shepherd"?"

"Oh no, David. I'm not really going to kill you. I'm only joking. Oh dear…"

And then he laughed. Of course, Miss was only joking.

In the Chapel, the Bishop would usually conduct the Mass. With his mitre and shepherd's crook, he cut an imposing figure. The Bishop was very inclusive, he seemed to understand the prisoners and their fears, and his homily always stressed the imperfections in all of us, prisoner and non-prisoner, all part of God's community, all part of the love of God. He wasn't patronising them, he was a humble man, and Kate knew he meant it.

The first carol…It had started. O Come all ye Faithful…With gusto! One hundred and eighty male voices singing "O come let us adore him…" with gusto! Fortissimo!

Then quiet for the readings.

In between "Gloria"…Oh the Gloria… Drums, guitars, piano, even a violin, the choir singing Glory, glory, glory to God… and the congregation replying…Glory to God, Glory to God, Spectacular!

More readings, the homily… more carols…While Shepherds watched their flocks by night…only, she noticed that some of her students were singing the "washed their socks" version, grinning mischievously.

The Communion, and "Silent Night". "Silent Night" and "Mary's Boy Child" sung by the choir. Sung beautifully. No more gusto, just so sweetly…You could hear a pin drop in the Chapel.

Finally, after the thanks from Father, the final carol…"Hark the Herald Angels Sing"… The music always seemed several octaves too high for Kate, and she ended up singing somewhere up in the Chapel ceiling, almost an out of body experience, as she tried to reach those high notes.

As the priests and bishop processed to the back of the chapel, the choir sang, "Do they know it's Christmas?" And it was over. The Sisters of Mercy, Mother Theresa's sisters gave out Christmas pictures to each of the men as they would begin to file out of the Chapel. Those around Kate were shaking hands, wishing each other a Merry Christmas. Kate tried to find her students, some of whom were still asking her about classes, even on Christmas Day. For some, maybe for all, from now on, this would be just another day.

One year, all Education was housed in R Wing. Kate had made her way across the wings to R Wing.

"Hi guys, hi...hi..." she called to them. They were all gathered around a large television down in the basement. "Happy Christmas, to all of you..."

"Miss, Miss, how are you...? Happy Christmas...What presents did you get? What did your husband get you? Was it what you wanted? When do you have your Christmas Dinner?"

She stopped to chat to each one...

Suddenly, a voice bellowed from the wing above:

"A woman...! A woman...! Thank you Father Christmas...! Thank you!"

A huge prisoner, with a big grin on his face, vaulted over the small gate separating the landings, bounded over to her, picked her up in a fireman's lift and started carrying her up the stairs.

Her students looked shocked. No one moved. Kate wondered, as one does, how much of her skirt had ridden up, in front of all these men. Not concerned that she was being taken away...in a fireman's lift...not concerned that she may be being taken hostage...not concerned about any of that...was her skirt now around her neck? Yes, a woman amongst all these men.

She turned round and looked pleadingly at her students over the shoulders of the "fireman". Their faces were a picture of indecision.

At the top of the stairs, her bulky "captor" put her down...

"Miss, Miss, Happy Christmas! Did I frighten you? I'm sorry, I'm sorry! Did I frighten you? Didn't mean to...Just a joke..."

"No, no of course not...hmmmm." Kate was smoothing down her skirt. "Happy Christmas to you."

When she went back to the class after Christmas, they all assured her that they were about to leap to her defence, but it was all right because the bulky one had put her down.

"Mmmmm, I didn't actually see any of you move. To my defence?...Mmmmm. Yes, I thought you might...only you were sort of...a long time..."

"No, no...we were just seeing what he was gonna do with you."

"God, that is so comforting, guys, so comforting...I knew I could depend on my students..."

"Oh Miss, really we were..."

What she loved about them was their good will. There was always good will. Sometimes, she doubted the good will, but they never let her down.

One day, she was walking along the wing, and came to the steep metal stairs. She was carrying books and folders and began climbing down the stairs. It was supper time, and all the prisoners in the wing were getting their food. Someone had dropped a dollop of custard on the stairs, and as she stepped onto the custard, she slipped, lost her balance, and crashed down the staircase. She knew that she must have been a sight for sore eyes, and waited for the guffaws, and the laughter.

For a split second, there was silence. Then a loud groan reverberated around the wing, and prisoners started running towards her. No one was laughing. They left their food and were running towards her.

"Miss, Miss, are you all right? Are you OK?" Hands reached out to her. People were lifting her up. "Miss, are you hurt? Can you move?"

"No, I'm fine, just a bit shaken…God, guys, I think I'm going to have a bruise to beat all bruises…"

"But have you broken anything? Do you need some help? Shall we get someone?"

"I'm fine, really, I just want to sit here for a while and feel sorry for myself…" she answered.

Some of them stayed with her, until she could get up. Then they helped her up and she continued on her way.

So, on Christmas Day, she could give back some of that good will. But then she would leave the prisoners and make her way home to her family and presents and drinks and turkey.

She would probably not think of the prisoners for the rest of the day. After all, for them it would be just another day. And she would be back on the day after Boxing Day and then it **would** be just another day.

Let's go, let's go

Prison can be a violent place. It must be terrifying when you first get there. There are bullies, and gangs and people like your cell mates who beat you up when the cell door closes, or who steal from you, and what do you do? What can you do?

Kate was making her way along the wing one day, when the alarm bell sounded. She backed herself against the wing wall, to leave space for the running officers. The sounds in the prison had become quite commonplace to her, but the whistle or the alarm bell going off never ceased to disturb her. Somewhere, either an officer or an inmate was in trouble, maybe being beaten severely or hurt in other ways, and the officers had to run despite the possibility of their running into trouble themselves. Horrific things happened, like boiling water sweetened with sugar which would stick better to the skin and which would then leave appalling burns. Or there were the batteries inside socks, which could beat you to death.

The Education Department was like a haven, a cocoon, and the teaching staff would rarely see true prison horror.

This time though, as Kate continued to walk down the wing, her cleaner came running up,

"Miss, Miss, it's Abdul... Abdul...He's been hurt..."

Abdul was one of her students.

"Hurt? How? Where is he now?" she asked.

"He's in the treatment room. He's hurt bad."

She hurried towards the treatment room.

Inside Abdul was lying on the treatment bed, with blood pouring out of his head. He had been attacked with a ripped can, so that the wounds were jagged. Chunks of his hair had been ripped out and the cuts were deep in his head and down his face. She did not have any gloves, so she had to be careful not to get any of his blood onto herself. The nurses were staunching the blood, and applying bandages and sutures.

But he was shaking badly from shock. She reached out for his hand.

"It's me, Abdul, it's Miss Kate. The nurses are here. You'll be OK."

He turned and looked at her, and gripped her hand tightly. A tear coursed down his cheek. He was so young.

"Abdul, I will get you a blanket. Hold on. We must get you warm," she was saying.

She ran out of the treatment room, and looked around for the green uniforms of the cleaners.

"Guys...get me some blankets...fast..."

"There are no blankets here, Miss, but we have some sheets..."

"Give me those, give me those..."

She took a pile of sheets and went back to Abdul. She tried not to get under the nurses' feet as they worked, but they did not complain. She wrapped Abdul in the sheets, like a mummy, and slowly he stopped shaking. She stayed there until he was ready to be taken to the hospital.

The next time she saw him, he was better. He came up to her on the wing and took her hand and kissed it.

"Thank you, Miss Kate..."

"Hey, don't thank me... I just got under everyone's feet, that's all. You take care."

Visitors to the Education Department did not see this side of the prison, and thought that the department reflected the civility of the whole place. She did not like to tell them that life was different on the wings, and it was not always so safe, but there was an awareness in the department too, about how quickly things could turn nasty, and the experienced teachers were quick to gauge when things were getting out of hand.

One day, Kate was called into a classroom, where two students were locked in a fierce, angry immobile stance. Both were holding each other by the hair, and both were so angry that they were actually crying with rage.

Kate unlocked their fingers from around the hair. They were separated, and led back to their wings.

Sometimes, things erupted so quickly and unexpectedly that even experienced teachers were shocked.

Kate had asked two of her students to work together at the computer. They were good friends, and usually worked together well. Suddenly, they both jumped up, ready to hit each other. She moved like lightning between them hoping that that would stop the aggression. They stood there facing each other over Kate's head, growling like wild animals.

"You don't call me stupid." It was like that film Kate had seen, where one bloke jumped up to fight another, shouting "Don't ever call me stupid".

Kate was glaring up at them from her place just at their chest height. She tried to get them to sit down. They would not. She knew that if she could get them to sit they would calm down, not feel so aggrieved, and they could be sorted.

They would not sit down.

So she ordered one to leave the classroom. He would not. She ordered the other one. No, he wouldn't either.

So she had to ask one of the other students to get the teacher from the other classroom to help.

Both of them tried to talk them down, and gradually, one teacher pulled one away one way, and the other, Kate, pulled the other way.

Then they were both marched back to their cells. Phewww.

Visitors too, particularly ones who came to do projects with the prisoners, would often take the credit for the good behaviour, somewhat galling to the teachers and to Kate, who had "trained" their students to behave well. There were also the usual "threats" issued by Kate which would be dished out before any project...and which generally followed the line that any misbehaviour towards the visitors would result in suspension, expulsion.....then death by slow means!

One day her Manager called Kate into the Department. A photographer from a newspaper was visiting and the Governor had asked if one of the teachers could help by escorting him around the wing. He wanted to take some photographs which were going to accompany an article in his paper.

She met him, but could see that he was going to be trouble.

"I have permission to go where I like." He sounded very arrogant.

"OK, but please follow what I say...please..."

"I have permission to go where I like…" She knew that he did not respect her judgement, and that somehow, to him permission meant safety. Hmmmmmm.

OK, thought Kate. Let's hope with this attitude he doesn't aggravate a prisoner.

They walked into the wing.

The Principal Officer greeted them, then called out to the prisoners:

"Listen up everyone!!! This gentleman is going to take some photographs. If you do not wish to have your photo taken, go now into your cells. If you don't mind having your photo taken, come into the Wing Office to sign a consent form."

"Now, is everyone clear? Go now into your cell if you do not want your photograph taken."

The photographer began taking photos. Click…prrr… click…prrr… Click…prrr… Photo after photo.

A prisoner came out of the shower. Click…prrr…

"Did you just take my picture, mate?"

"I've got permission," Journalist mate replied confidently.

"You ain't got permission to take my picture…what you doing?"

Kate could smell trouble brewing.

"I think you should come with me out of this wing, now…" she said anxiously to the photographer.

The prisoner stormed into the wing office.

"Guv, what's he playing at? He just took my picture?"

The Principal Officer realised that this prisoner had been in the shower when the instructions about the photographs were given out.

"Sorry mate," he said to the photographer, "I'm afraid there's been a slight mistake. I need your camera, and I will have to destroy the photos you've taken."

"But, I've got permission."

"No, I'm sorry, this prisoner did not hear my instructions about having photos taken...I need your camera...then you can start taking all the photographs you want, but those first ones have to be destroyed..."

"But..."

The prisoner had now gone out into the wing and was shouting to the others:

"I'm goin' to have his guts. You see if I don't...take my picture? Huh...who does he think he is?"

"I'll give you the camera," said the photographer wisely.

When the spool of film was removed, he came back into the wing, ready to take more photos.

"Hey, I told you...I'm going to get your guts, mate..." the prisoner was still angry. "You don't take a picture of me, then think that that's OK...and argue with me that it's OK..."

Kate was telling the photographer that they should remove themselves and fast...

"But... but...he can't tell me what to do..."

Kate was becoming desperate. They could do without trouble in the wing. This silly man was totally unaware that he was putting himself and the wing staff in jeopardy.

"Look mate, if you don't get off this wing, like NOW…I'm going to…do your head in…" The prisoner continued to shout and gesticulate, to anyone listening.

"Please, come with me, now," said Kate. "He's threatened you in front of his mates, he will not want to lose face…you can get your photographs in another wing…I'm really warning you now…you must do as I say."

He came. He followed Kate. Thank God. And God save us and protect us from idiots who visit the prison, thought Kate.

He got his photographs elsewhere.

Kate went back to the Manager…

"Hey, did you think that that was going to be an easy afternoon for me…?" asked Kate.

"Why, what could be difficult about escorting a photographer…?"

"Don't ask…don't even ask…"

Hostage

"OK Dan, how are you today?"

Kate was doing some one-to-one work with Dan in B Wing.

Dan had problems with reading and writing and needed some individual help. Individual help, because whatever they did, and however much they encouraged, Dan would not go to Education.

Poor Dan, he was afraid of his own shadow. Clearly, someone with a personality disorder and a social phobia, or just embarrassed that he couldn't read and write. He needed help, so Kate came down to him every other day.

"Yes, Miss, I'm fine."

"OK, today, we will learn five spellings, and read another two pages of that thriller."

It was not much of a thriller, not much of a "page turner", because it only contained three letter words or words which could be broken into three-letter syllables, with a few "most-used" words in between. However, what Kate wanted was for Dan, for the first time in his life, to be introduced to reading as it should be. In other words, she wanted Dan to want to read, to want to know what happens next, so that he would begin to understand what this reading "malarkey" was all about.

"Shall we read first?"

"Yep, Miss…we got to that bit where they find the body…"

"God, yes, a bod…y with…out a head…" She found herself talking in syllables to Dan. Maybe people always talked to him in syllables, and maybe he thought that the whole English language was made up of words which are spoken syllable by syllable. Maybe her legacy to poor Dan would be that he learnt to speak that way...God forbid.

"There was the bod...y...with...out the head. Who had the head? said Ben. And why did he kill this man?" Dan read slowly, "Was this a man who liked to kill? Did he kill many other people? De...tec...tive Ben looked at his chum..." Chum, chum? thought Kate, well, by the time he leaves the prison, Dan will not only speak in three-letter syllabics but be a walking Thesaurus of three-letter, one-syllable silly words...great!

"Ben said, "I think we should see what we can f...f...f..."

"OK, Dan, what is this word, we learnt it last time...?" She wrote it down. "What did we say you were when people asked you for cigarettes?"

"Stupid."

"No." Oh dear. "Kind...kind...because you give everyone a cigarette...that's generous...kind...that's what we said you were...kind."

"Yes, Miss...kind..."

"Now what is this sound? Mmmmmm."

"Mmmmmm..."

"Yes...now try mmmm...ind."

"Mmmmmm...ind..." he mimicked.

He was not going to get the word.

"It's MIND, MIND...it sounds like kind, and look it looks like kind..."

Blank face...It didn't look like "kind" to Dan.

"OK, this word is ffffff........ind...so... OK, it's ffff....ind...I think we should find, find...the...go on..."

"I think we should find the kill...er on the com...com...com."

"What does a detective use to find killers?"

"Dunno, Miss...I've never been a detective..."

"A computer...He has names on a computer which match what he's looking for."   A very slow page turner, this. "OK..."

"I   think   we   should   find   the   kill...er...on   a com...puuuuuu...ter."

"Good, good." She was never impatient with her Basic Skills learners, as it was so hard for them...what an uphill struggle! They needed all the encouragement she could give them.

"To see if there is a kill...er who chops off heads. De...tec...tive...Ben went to the com...com..."

"Yes, Dan...com...what? Com..." She pretends to tap on a keyboard

"Computer, Miss, computer."

"Yes. Well done."

"We   have   to   stop   this   kill...er   be...fore...he   kills a...gain...How will they stop him with the computer, Miss?"

"Ummm, well, they won't stop him. They'll find out who he is and arrest him. I think...Let's see what the story says...I may be wrong..."

They struggled through the page. "The computer does not have any...one who chops off heads, so this is a new kill...er. So this is some...one new. They have to find him be...fore he kills again..."

"So, now what do they do, Miss? Cos the computer doesn't help."

"Aaahhh, you see, we have to read and see. What will they do next? A haaaa..."

Reading, reading...Now she hopes that Dan will try to work out, or ask someone, what Detective Ben does to find the killer. Now, she hopes that Dan begins to taste what reading a story is about...even if it's about head chopping...How appropriate for a prison class!

"Now, we're going to write. We're going to write a play."

"A play, Miss, ha ha..."

"OK, Mr. Dan, where would you like to go on holiday?"

"Paris, Miss. Paris."

"Paris, wow. OK, who will you go with?"

"Jeff, my brother Jeff."

"Where will you stay?"

"A posh hotel...in Paris."

"What will you do there?"

"Hmmm, Miss..."

"Keep it clean, Dan, keep it clean...God, what I have to put up with." Dan laughed.

"I'll keep it clean, just for you, Miss. I'll go out to a café in Paris."

"And...what else will you do?"

"I'll keep it clean, Miss...I'll walk".

"Great, so let's write all that down...Dan wants to go to Paris for his holiday with his brother Jeff. They want to go to cafés and walk. Can you read it back to me?"

"Now, Mr Dan...we're going to write the play...We're in a café with Jeff in Paris...I am Jeff and you are Dan...

Hi Dan..."

"Hi Jeff..."

"Are you enjoying this holiday in Paris, Dan?"

"Yep..."

"Go on, go on, you can't just say yep...plays aren't like that..."

At the end of the morning they have a story, a play. Dan has learnt to spell some of the words that he would say to his brother Jeff on holiday in Paris and Dan wants to know what Detective Ben is going to do next.

"OK, see you on Thursday, Dan. Well done."

She enjoyed teaching Basic Skills and went back to the Department, feeling she had achieved a lot.

Next morning her manager wanted to see her.

"The Principal Officer of B Wing wants to speak to you. Go and see him at lunchtime. What's happened?"

She went to B Wing. The PO sat her down.

"You teach Daniel?"

"Why, what's happened?"

"It's come to us across the prison grapevine, that Daniel is going to take you hostage tomorrow, Thursday, morning."

"Daniel? Daniel?" She couldn't believe it. He wouldn't say "boo to a goose", and he was planning to take her hostage?

"He won't do that, honestly. He wouldn't think like that," she said.

"So, do you intend to come and teach him as usual tomorrow?"

"Yes. He just wouldn't. I can't believe it."

She went back to the Department.

Her Manager tried to dissuade her from going on Thursday. But she wouldn't be dissuaded. Daniel wouldn't take anyone hostage. Daniel?

She went home that evening.

In the middle of the night, it didn't look so rosy. The door to that office was shut. If he blockaded her in, what would he do to her? She didn't know what he was in for, but she began to be afraid. What if he raped her? Or hurt her? Was he special? Did he have mental health issues?

She came into work the next day, and tried to laugh.

"Well, I suppose I'd better put my make up on so that I look good on the news tonight. Should I cry when I'm rescued, or should I laugh hysterically?" she asked her Manager.

The Manager insisted on going down to B Wing with her, and tried again to dissuade her.

They walked down to B Wing, along one wing, across the centre, and down A, towards B Wing. Kate was feeling more and more afraid. Maybe this wasn't such a good idea, after all.

They opened the Gates to B Wing. The office where she taught was open. There was a chair in the doorway, and sitting in the chair, an officer.

"Well, you didn't think we were going to take a blind bit of notice of you," said the Principal Officer. "What's more, you will not be teaching Daniel after today, as he is being shipped out tomorrow." She knew that she couldn't tell Daniel, and she knew she would miss her classes with him, but when she looked reality in the face, it was not a pretty sight, and she didn't want to be afraid every time she came here.

Daniel came in. He was surprised that there was an officer sitting with them all morning, but did not comment.

Kate tried to be natural but in effect watched his every move like a hawk. She didn't really believe that he was capable of taking her hostage...but...

Hell, it was OK to be brave now that it was all over.

There is No One Else

"Miss, why are you having a go at me again? You're always having a go at me." Andy was a student from well, not hell exactly, but certainly purgatory. He was always arguing with her and the others, and if crossed, even slightly, would dispute the issue and argue and argue. He couldn't let anything go. Belligerent, aggressive, argumentative, confrontational…a pleasant student, then.

"Because I hate you," replied Kate smiling sweetly. "There can be no other reason, because you are such a lovely person, so quiet, so reasonable, so lovable, so I argue with you because I hate you…There you are, that's the reason."

He laughed despite himself, "Miss, you know I can't do this work. You know I can't do it…So why are you making me?"

"Because, my little angel…from hell…I hate you. And I have decided that making you work on your English exercises, so that you can pass your exams, so that you can make something of yourself when you leave this place…will cause you suffering, and that is why… Now get on with your work and stop whingeing."

She had to admit that when he was released she was relieved.

A few months later, the Manager wanted to see her.

"I've had a phone call from a Probation Officer about your dreadful Andy. He was involved in an argument outside a pub, had a fight, then went away, and came back later with a weapon and killed the bloke he argued with."

"Oh my God, how stupid, how stupid. Why on earth can't he hold his temper? Why on earth…why on earth…?"

"Well," the Manager continued, "he's waiting for trial, for murder, premeditated, so that will probably be Life. His family have rejected him totally. They don't want anything to do with him. He has no one now and he's suicidal. His Probation Officer asked him if he has any friends at all, and he said that he doesn't. Except one person...he has one friend...Kate...you! His English teacher..."

"Me, I'm not his friend. Me? We were always at each other's throat. How can he say I'm his friend? He must be mad. I tried to be his teacher and that was hard enough. Friend?" But there was something so very sad, so heartbreakingly sad that Andy considered her his friend, because he had no one else in the world. So his teacher, his prison teacher was his only friend. And yet, now he'd *murdered* someone, killed another human being...oh God...

"So," continued her Manager. "Because you are his only friend (?) the Probation Officer wondered if you could write to him occasionally, so that he doesn't feel so isolated. I think it would be a good idea if you checked all the letters you send with me, so that everything is above board, and you are covered."

"Oh God, I don't know if I can write to him. I just feel that that is a bad idea. If he has no one, he will become attached and that would be very dangerous, you know that."

"OK, I'll let them know."

"Oh God, I can't just leave him though. I'll write."

So she wrote and Andy wrote back. She would write to him as she had talked to him, "bullying" him not to give up, and certainly not to entertain taking his own life.

He got Life and was moved to a Lifers prison.

She continued to write to him. He would write back telling her about how the Education Department there didn't suit him. I bet it didn't, she thought, nothing really suited Andy.

He wrote to tell her that he had fallen in love with his probation officer in the prison. She wrote to tell him that that was not a good thing, as it wasn't really love, but a longing for love.

He wrote to tell her that that's what *they, psychology* had told him and she wrote back to tell him that he would be hurt, whichever way he played it.

He wrote to tell her that the psychologist said that he had a problem with women and she wrote back to tell him to be mature about all this and to look at the reality.

He wrote to tell her that he could see that she was right, and he was trying to be mature. She wrote and wondered if he had changed...mature? But however cynical and sarcastic she was to him, he kept up the correspondence. Clearly, she was still all he had, despite everything.

Then she was asked to start a new course in the department: A Start your Own Business Course. The only other prison doing this course was the prison where Andy was serving his Life Sentence.

She had to go to the prison, but her dilemma was whether to visit Andy while she was there, or whether not to mention anything to him.

He had changed, it was true. He did seem to be more mature. He was getting help from psychologists and others; maybe it would be nice to see him, and he would be pleased that she had bothered. A short twenty minute visit wouldn't hurt her.

On the other hand, he saw her as his friend and she wasn't his friend. They had so far only corresponded, which was safe;

meeting him was a different "ball game". If he became attached to her, he would be hurt again, and she could not allow that. Kate always believed that the prisoners were in the care of the staff, and so it was extremely important to be aware of their vulnerability, and not to "toy" with their feelings in any way.

She mulled over everything. Which was kinder, to visit or not to visit? Maybe it would be easier to ask herself what good would it do? If she visited him, he would feel that there was at least one person in the world who wanted to see him, and that would help his self-esteem. If she didn't visit him, he would never know, so it wouldn't hurt.

Eventually, she rang the prison, and asked the probation officer for his advice. He said that it would be good for Andy to be visited, as yes, it had been difficult for him to adjust to his Life sentence, and that they were indeed making progress with his rehabilitation.

So, she asked the Probation Officer to make the arrangements and she wrote to Andy to say she was coming to his prison.

He was delighted, and was looking forward to her visit.

She told him not to expect too much and that she was only "popping in" to see him as her primary motive to visit the prison was to learn about running a Start Your Own Business class.

The train to the prison took some hours and she prepared her questions to the Education Department there, but despite it not being her primary reason to visit, Kate couldn't help but worry about visiting Andy.

She could not avoid an intuitive feeling that gnawed away at her. The feeling would not go away. Her instincts told her that it was going to be a huge mistake to visit Andy.

Nevertheless, her other instincts said that it would be good to see him and to talk about his progress. Anyway it was too late now...

She visited the Education Department and then asked the teacher to take her to the Lifers' Wing. The Principal Officer invited her into his office and went to fetch Andy.

Oh, he was so pleased to see her. He hadn't changed one bit. He was the same belligerent Andy but he couldn't help himself and laughed and laughed at her silly jokes.

She told him about this new course, and how she knew nothing about business. She'd had this wild idea that it would be a good course to start, as it would give people an opportunity to do something with their lives, but she knew nothing about business.

He told her about his psychology courses, and how everyone was pleased with him.

She stayed for twenty minutes and then got up to go. He didn't want her to go. She made him laugh, and it was going to be lonely without her. But she insisted. She would write, but she had to get back now.

The next day, there was a phone call from Andy. He wanted to see her again.

No, she couldn't come to see him and he wasn't to phone. It would be better to write.

Another day, another phone call. Why couldn't she see him?

Because she couldn't. The Home Office didn't allow her to see him and anyway, it was not a good idea.

He complained to the Home Office. He wrote complaint after complaint.

She told the administrator that she would not answer his phone calls, so she told him not to bother to phone.

She wrote and told him that she would not go and see him; even if he got three million permissions from the Home Office, she would... Not... Go...To... See... Him!

He wrote back asking why...

Because professionally, she did not have time to go and visit all her ex-students.

He wrote back and told her that he was not telling her to go and visit *all* her ex-students. They may not need to see her. He did.

She wrote back to tell him that it wasn't a question of what he wanted or needed, she had a family to look after, her job was her job, and it did not entail visiting him.

Gradually the letters became less desperate and less frequent, and finally, after about a year, Andy was moved to yet another prison, and his letters stopped altogether.

Kate knew that she should have taken notice of her intuition. She hoped that she hadn't hurt Andy, but what was truly sad was how much he had needed love and affection, like everyone else in the world, only, he had no one in the world to give it to him.

Whatever and however, love and affection are redemptive. She hoped that Andy would find that love, and eventually be happy.

A New Department

Gradually over the years, the prison eased some of the rules and tightened others.

Initially, the remand prisoners waiting for trial were to be kept separate from the sentenced prisoners, which in effect meant that the sentenced prisoners could attend Education but the remand prisoners were getting none.

Finally, it was decided that the remand prisoners would get classes and Education was given a set of rooms, above the workshops.

Kate was Acting Deputy Manager at the time, so she was given the task of opening the new Department.

It was not much. Five tiny classrooms, with a store room off one of them, and a tiny office/staffroom, but it was something.

The new department would mirror the old one. They would have to have an Art/Pottery Room, a Basic Skills room, an English/Maths room, an ESOL (English for Speakers of Other Languages) class and a Computer class.

Whilst Kate arranged for the cleaners to clear out the store room, and for the Co-ordinators of Departments to resource the new classrooms, she chose a feisty teacher, Linda, to help her and they both set out to recruit students.

The remand prisoners lived in one wing. It was a huge wing and housed about one hundred of them. They had nothing better to do all day but stay in their cells, or go and watch television on the days they had association and spend an hour each day on exercise. She and Linda thought that their task would be easy. The prisoners would be bored, wanting desperately to get out of their cells and into Education.

They prepared posters inviting people to apply for the new Education classes: brilliant, spanking new Education classes! In these classes, people would be given a chance to brush up on their Education, learn new skills in Computing, explore their talent in Art and Pottery, and what is more, get a nationally recognised accreditation to take out with them, which would help them, hopefully, to find a job. There was always a huge waiting list for the other Education classes, so students would come streaming in, wouldn't they?

Nobody applied. Nobody wanted to come to Education! Bright, colourful posters, and no one took any notice of them. There was a danger that they would have their brilliant, spanking new classes, with brilliant, spanking new resources and…no students.

OK, what was going wrong? Perhaps people had not seen them. There was an awful lot of paperwork displayed in the wings, and people could have missed their posters.

Kate and Linda moved the posters nearer the food-serving hatches. That was bound to attract some recruits. They could not miss the posters now.

Nothing… no recruits. Clearly, it was not "fashionable" to come to Education.

How to make it more "trendy", more "fashionable"?

The posters would have to change: Do you want a job on the outside? Do you need to brush up on your Maths and English? Do you want to develop new talents? Don't you want to learn new computing skills, which will hold you in good stead on the outside? Linda and Kate would appeal to their aspirations.

Only, they didn't seem to have any. They were wallowing in apathy and despair. They were waiting for their trial and had no motivation to do anything other than what they were told. They were institutionalised before they had even started their prison life.

What to do? Linda and Kate decided to appeal to the "leaders". Kate always felt that the prison population was made up of "leaders" and "sheep". Unfair, but it mirrored society outside. If the "leaders" thought education was good, the "sheep" would follow. The "leaders" at least would have some aspirations, even if the "sheep" had lost all theirs. Generally, prisoners would find some way of doing their "time" and the "leaders" were often those who had been in prison before and knew their way around. They would know how to try to make the sentence pass more easily, and those who were undecided or inexperienced would see which path to follow as it might turn out to be the easier path.

They went out into the wing and spoke to the cleaners. Theirs was a good job. It got them out of their cells, it gave them certain privileges, such as having a cup of tea when they wished, and generally they were much "freer" than their prison mates. They were "leaders".

"Hey, guys. We're trying to get people to come to the new Education Department. No one wants to come. Any ideas?"

"Give them incentives, Miss. Pay them." The cleaners got paid. £5 a week, not much… but better than not being paid at all.

"Yes, but we have no money to pay them."

"You won't get anyone into Education unless you give them incentives…you will have to pay them."

"Well, we're trying to encourage people to come for their own good. Education will give them a stepping stone into the world outside."

"You see, Miss...there are ways of doing your bird and there are ways of doing your bird. Having money for cigarettes, a bit of extra food, and say a cup of coffee every now and then, and some nice soap and toothpaste, not that stuff they give you in here...well, that's an incentive, and makes the time go easier."

Well, it probably did, but Linda and Kate had no money for that sort of incentive. Even the students in the main Education Department were paid less than their fellow prisoners in the workshops.

"No can do..."

So, Linda and Kate were back to square one.

"There's only one way", said Kate. "We'll have to do what they used to do on the old sailing ships..."

"God, Kate, you don't mean we will have to press gang them...God, I don't think that will work. We can't just go into the wings rounding them up. "Hi guys, come with me...oh and by the way, you are now in Education"...what are you thinking of?"

"No, not as bad as that...but we'll have to recruit them personally. Only way."

"How, the hell are we going to do that?"

"Watch, see and learn, watch, see and learn."

Kate armed herself with application forms and her brightest smile, and with Linda they went into the Association Room.

The Association Room was a large room off D Wing. Half the room was furnished with easy chairs and a television. Here also was a canteen where you could exchange your canteen form for any goods, such as coffee, tea, soap and biscuits. And finally, in one corner there was some Gym equipment and pool tables... So, not much competition for Education there...?

Kate and Linda walked in looking more confident than they felt. The room was full of prisoners, very hostile-looking prisoners. They were watching some film with Kirk Douglas...or was it Tony Curtis? He was a Viking warrior of some sort and was fighting his way through the film. People were lounging in the easy chairs, half asleep. Some were not watching the film, but were playing pool and some were using Gym Equipment. These looked slightly more animated and not as hostile as those watching the television.

Kate pushed her way along the last row of easy chairs.

"Hi guys, I'm from Education. Yes, I know I'm in your way, but what are you doing wasting your life in here...Watching a boring film...Yes, this one may not be boring, but watching a film every single day must drive you potty..."

She was not well received, and was getting the "evil eye". Hostility was an understatement, but she was not going to give in so easily. What is a little hostility, after all? What was the worst that could happen?

Linda understood what Kate was trying to do, and started at the other end of the row.

"Come on, just one class will not hurt you. It might do you some good...come on...you could get a certificate for Computing...how about that? "

There was muttering and in all fairness, you could say without exaggeration, that they were both not very popular. In fact, without exaggerating, you could even say that they were extremely unpopular. Still, there really wasn't anything much worse than a few mild expletives (the prisoners did not swear in front of the Education female staff), and some muttering and maybe some vicious staring. Nothing put off those two.

"Come on, just one class. Here's an application form. Go on, go on. Try it, it won't bite."

They moved up the rows. Some of the guys were filling in one class. Result! Once a few had agreed to come, more were interested.

Slowly, slowly, they were getting a few people to come to Education.

"And if I don't like it, can I come off?"

"Course, we're not forcing you to do anything, but you'll like it, you'll see. We're nice in Education. Honest. You will like it…"

By the end of the morning they had about twenty recruits.

Back in the department, they jumped around like demented chickens…

"Result, result!!! Let's get these on the Unlocking lists and get them started for tomorrow."

Next day…more results…

"Come on, come on…soon there won't be room on the classes and you won't be able to choose…"

Those who had come to the classes were indeed pleased…and signed on for more.

Linda and Kate had ammunition…

"You see... those who went on Wednesday, can you see them here? No, you can't. No... You... Can't...because...? Because they haven't come back...they haven't come back... And why haven't they come back...? Because what we told you is true...once you have tried education, you won't look back...you will want more..."

They weren't always successful, and there were some who came and didn't come again, but the majority stayed. They became interested and motivated. They wanted "certificates". They began to lose that dreadful apathy that invades prison life.

At last came the day when the database showed a waiting list...Yessss. Hooray for Education and the students!!! They did not have to recruit any longer...The classes were full to bursting, and they had done what they had set out to do.

Several years later, the remand and sentenced prisoners were allowed to work together, and so one Education Department was allocated to those who had higher level scores in Literacy and Numeracy and could work right up to A Levels and even, when the local University became involved, could do Access Courses to University; and the other was allocated to the ones needing help with Basic Skills in Literacy and Numeracy and support to those with Dyslexia. What is more, the Education students were paid, all of them, and at the same rate as the workshops.

But it had started small...and grew...and grew...

Sit on Your Hands

There had been a Health class in the department, but the teacher had left a while ago, and there was no class to replace it.

The Education Manager asked Kate if she could start a new Health class.

"But...but...I don't know anything about Health. Do I look as if I know anything about Health? In fact, I look pretty unhealthy...to say the least...They won't be very impressed with someone teaching them about health, who looks as if, she herself is about to enter death's door, now, will they?" Kate put on her sad, put-upon face.

It didn't do any good.

"No, you can do it. Look, here's a text book. It's even got exercises."

Kate was still very dubious. She was going to start a class. Keep the guys interested and motivated. Teach them things that they needed to know. But she hadn't a clue what and how to teach it.

"I don't think I can, really I don't..." she protested.

"Yes, you can. A teacher should be able to teach anything. It's not the subject, as you know, but the skill of presenting a subject well, which makes a good teacher. And you have those skills, you know you do. A teacher should be able to teach anything. Just learn a little about health...nothing could be easier."

"I suppose you're right, but I'm still not all that sure I can..."

"What's more," the Education Manager continued, ignoring all protests, "the prison would like you to give them some sex education, sexually transmitted diseases, contraception, that sort of thing…"

"Nooooo…I won't do sex education…I can't…I can't do health, and I certainly can't teach sex education…me, a woman…to a bunch of guys…noooo…I can't…"

So, here she was in a bookshop looking for books on sex.

She'd persuaded her seven-year old daughter to come with her, because she had convinced herself that the service person at the counter would think she was a pervert, or certainly someone with an unhealthy interest in sex, who was buying an awful lot of sex books. So, having a seven-year old running about calling her mum, might change their opinion of her. It didn't help that she was creeping about, looking for and at books very surreptitiously, and constantly asking her daughter if anyone was watching. She should have worn a dirty mac, she thought to herself.

"But mum, the lady didn't even look at the covers of the books you bought," said her long-suffering offspring, "she just put the thing down the stripes, and wasn't looking at what you bought. And anyway, why are you so scared about people seeing what you're buying?"

Yes, why? It didn't bode well for the class, if their teacher was so embarrassed by *buying* the books. How embarrassed would she be by delivering the content in them? Hmmmmm?

OK, she prepared the scheme of work for the course. There was healthy eating, healthy exercise, healthy living, healthy sex…healthy sex… healthy sex? Was she getting obsessed? She prepared lesson plans for each of the subjects.

She made an appointment to go to the Family Planning Clinic, where she asked for some leaflets and contraceptives.

She went to her GP and picked up some more leaflets about smoking, alcohol abuse and help with various diseases.

She asked the prison hospital to give her some lessons in First Aid.

So, she had the scheme of work, lesson plans, resources, a suspicion that she was already suffering from all the diseases in the leaflets (why did she do that…all it needed was a peek at any medical book and Kate was away…death from every disease under the sun) and now she had to have confidence to teach the course.

Lesson One. Are You Healthy? She'd start with a bang!

Are You Healthy? A good place to start in a prison, where they had no real influence over whether they were healthy or not, and relied on the prison somewhat to provide them with healthy food, healthy exercise, healthy sleep, a healthy life style. Would they accuse her of having a laugh, or would her first class in health spark off a mountain of complaints about the food or a long queue to see the doctor?

She started by having them all take their pulse, then running up and down like demented ones, then taking their pulse again to see if they had a regular pulse, and to see if they were out of condition. The final result showed that *they* were pretty healthy, but she wasn't. Her pulse rate was much too high.

"You should be more careful, Miss…"

Who was taking this class, anyway?

What made it worse was that whilst they were jumping up and down and running around the class, she caught a glimpse of some visitors and the Governor outside in the corridor looking through the windows into the classroom, with decidedly puzzled expressions on their faces. When she spotted them outside, she opened the door and told the visitors that she was doing health…protesting too much?

"It was those visitors coming round that made my pulse so high, guys. I am an incredibly healthy person…so there…"

Now the class was looking decidedly puzzled.

The following week they looked at food, and its nutrients…They made charts and tables and diaries and… and…. and….by the time she had finished with them and this course, these guys would be able to move mountains. Healthy? By God, they would be!

Next lesson. First aid. She'd brought Resuscie Annie from the hospital, and they were going to practise saving Annie.

"Right guys, Annie's had an accident. You are the only one there. What do you think you should do first? Good, Richard…ring 999, as quickly as you can…then you can start trying to help Annie.

It's no good your helping Annie if you're in a state, so you must calm yourself…no, you don't need a spliff…thank you very much, Damian…that is *not* a good idea at the best of times, and this is a health class, Damian, we do not think in terms of grass or any other unnecessaries in here… Yes, I know you are only pretending, but even to think…well…

Now you've calmed down and gathered your thoughts together…

A…B…C…guys. Remember A…B…C…

Check her airways first…she might have something down her throat which is restricting her breathing…Look I will show you how…Don't ram your hand down her throat…just use your fingers, like this…now you all try…good…good…

Then, check her breathing. Is she breathing? Well, of course, she isn't, she's a doll...thank you Leslie...we knew that already....

So, what have you done so far to help her? Good...

She is still not breathing...you have to work on her chest...can you see how I'm measuring where I should start...And we have to breathe into her mouth, so that her chest inflates...like that."

They were doing well.

She summarised the lesson and went to pick up Annie. Leslie, her comedian had got there first, and was making the others laugh by not letting go of Annie...Oh dear...there was always one...

"Leslie, get off Annie..."

God, it only needed the Governor to come round again with his visitors, and he would have her certified.

"Leslie..!"

Then. The sex education lesson.

"Guys, I'm going to do some sex education with you today."

There was general frivolity at that introduction (she expected nothing less)...hmmm, sex education? They, the big machos, would need none of that...Miss!

"OK, you, my little students, are going to sit on your hands, while I take this lesson." Well, she was not going to have *that* sort of behaviour in her class, was she?

"Miss, Miss, what are you saying? Why?" There was an outcry.

"Now, on your hands…now…"

They did as they were told. They did look sweet. All perched on their hands.

"OK, first we're going to look at some diagrams of the sexual organs of a man and a woman. I want you to label the bits I've indicated on the diagrams. This is going to be confidential, guys. I am going to take in these diagrams and see how much you know about the way a man and a woman are put together…very funny, Leslie…very funny…So, I'm not going to laugh, well not much anyway, at your pathetic knowledge about the female form…and how little you know…Uh Uh…sit on your hands.

Now, you do not have to put your names on the diagrams, so that even I won't know who the diagrams belong to, and then there won't be any embarrassment.

You can remove your hands, fill in the diagrams then sit on your hands again. OK?"

The class was enjoying themselves. Well, they would, wouldn't they? There was little attempt at confidentiality, and the answers were group efforts, which was fine, because she did not want to humiliate individuals.

When they were all sitting back on their hands again…she continued the lesson.

"OK guys, so what happens when you use some of these contraceptives I'm going to show you? How does each of these contraceptives work on the body? Before we do that though, I will have to show you how the condom works. Bit messy, but let's go… This is how you put one on."

They were following what she was saying intently. What is more, neither she nor they were embarrassed any longer. She had become the equivalent of someone medical, and they trusted her, as they would a doctor. How extraordinary.

She told them about sexually transmitted diseases, the myths, the legends and most importantly the consequences of getting them and how to avoid doing this by using contraception.

They asked her intimate questions, which they trusted her to answer.

She showed them an intimate film, produced by the prison service, which emphasised all the more about diseases.

By the time Kate had taught her Health class several times, she was not even embarrassed to talk about sex outside of the classroom. In fact, she was in danger of becoming blasé about the whole thing.

But whenever she came to the sex education, they would have to start by sitting on their hands. It made them laugh, it helped them become comfortable with her and her with them. It stopped any embarrassment, and she hoped that in the long term it may have helped them stay healthy and not get diseases.

Poland

Kate's parents were Polish and Kate and her husband and son were going to visit Poland.

"You have to fill in a form," her Education Manager told her. "You have to fill in a form that you won't get involved in any black market activities."

Yes, yes, thought Kate. They were all making fun of her trip to the darkness of Communist Poland.

"Will we see you again?" asked her students…"You'll probably be sent to a gulag."

Ha ha ha…

"At least you can see what their Education Department is like…"

Ha ha ha…

"Knowing Miss, she'll probably start changing it…"

Ha ha ha….

"Don't worry, Miss, we'll visit you…"

HA HA HA…

She did not sign any forms. She did not believe her Manager. It was 1978… What could go wrong?

They were going to Poland by car, with a stop-off at a hotel in Magdeburg in East Germany. All was above board…They had their visa for East Germany and their visa for Poland. Black market activities? Ha ha ha! As if…

They crossed the border between East and West Germany. A three-hour delay while their paperwork, cars and they themselves, were checked and checked and checked. It was daunting somehow to move across the no-man's land under the watching towers with their soldiers holding guns, pointing straight at them.

Eventually, they were on the motorway again towards Magdeburg.

Magdeburg turned out to be a very pleasant city, and they found their hotel easily. Oh, for a shower, a meal, and a good night's sleep. Their son, only two years old, had become quite fractious by then, and they all needed a rest.

Only not yet, it seemed. They went to register at reception.

Yes, they had a visa...? Of course, they had a visa... It was a transit visa...? What did that mean...? They couldn't stop in East Germany... They **what**? ... But they had got their visa in London... They had been assured that they could stop in East Germany...

No, they would have to go back to the border and get another visa.

No, they wouldn't, said Kate's husband... They were going to stay in this hotel... They were going to have a meal and they were going to put their son to bed... There was nothing on earth that would persuade them to go back to the border.

The lady looked worried. She would have to phone the police.

Oh great...they hadn't even got to Poland and they were going to be sent to a gulag, thought Kate. Great.

"Keep smiling to the policeman," she said to her husband…
"Just keep smiling. I really don't want to stay in an East
German police cell…this "ain't" England…"

Her husband was determined. He was extremely sorry to
cause trouble… It had not been their fault…They had booked
the hotel and got the visa in the East German Travel Bureau in
London…It was *their* fault, and it would be dreadful to drag a
little two-year old, who was extremely tired, all the way back
to the border…

OK, they were in…The policeman relented.

The next morning… Another border, another communist
check…

The Polish border. They had to declare how much English
money they were taking into Poland, and they were going to
have to declare how much they had spent in Poland with
receipts to prove it, on the way back…Thank God for
bureaucracy, thought Kate, it made the holiday so much more
interesting.

As they moved away from the customs, her husband reached
down and took out a wad of pound notes from under the mat
at his feet.

"Nooo…" Kate was horrified. "We ain't in England…" They
were going to end up in a gulag, of that there was no doubt.
"Why didn't you tell me?"

"You'd have given the game away immediately…" her
husband told her.

Well, at least she hadn't had to lie and look guilty.

They drove into the first town, and stopped at the traffic
lights.

There was a knock on the window.

Kate slid the window down.

"Have you got any dollars?" the man asked her.

"Dollars, absolutely not." He was probably an agent provocateur, or something. She was getting paranoid.

There was a "clever" system in Poland. They had two sets of shops, the ones which sold goods (if there were any) for Polish money and the ones (Pewex) which sold goods, like washing machines, televisions, etc, for hard currency. The Poles needed the hard currency to buy anything.

So, this was their introduction to Poland!

It wasn't so bad, and they would soon be with her family, who would take care of them.

Then they lost her son's pushchair. Great. They stopped to have a picnic and left it by the roadside.

Well, never mind, such is life. They were going to a big city, Szczecin, and they would have to get another pushchair there.

It was wonderful to see her family again. She hadn't seen them for at least ten years.

A pushchair...oh dear...there was nowhere selling pushchairs...

Nowhere...? Nowhere...? Didn't they have big department stores? Didn't they have anything...?

The department store they went to was almost bare...certainly no pushchairs. Even in hard currency? Nope...nothing like that.

OK. They would have to manage. Their next stop was Wrocław...a bigger city...sure to have pushchairs. In the meantime they would have to carry their son.

Wrocław...Another city, another problem. Kate's uncle was a colonel in the Polish army... They were to be extremely careful and not to indicate in any way that they were from England. That would be very dangerous. They would have to park the car on the outskirts of the city, and come to her family's apartment by tram. Kate's husband was not to say a word in English. Kate could speak Polish, so she had to pretend that they were a visiting family from another part of Poland. They stayed for a few days, even went for a tour of Wrocław, without admitting once that they were, in fact, from England. God, they really did not appreciate how easy life was back home. But, so far, so good. It was lovely to see the family.

They went to a department store in Wrocław. Pushchairs? Pushchairs? Really, thought Kate, did the lovely bureaucrats up there in Warsaw think that no one needed pushchairs in this country? Maybe that was their system of birth control. No pushchairs, so no babies, so no pushchairs...so, no babies! Hmmmm.

A woman came up to her in the store.

"Madam, they have a shipment of Russian pushchairs just come in, at a bazaar on the outskirts. Take tram 32, and it should take you right to the bazaar. You should get a pushchair there...but hurry."

Sure enough. Russian pushchairs. The handles were so weak that they bent, but at least they had a pushchair.

Wherever they went everyone wanted pounds. Her family had been waiting for them to come so that they could exchange their złotys for "proper" money.

"Hard currency, have you got any pounds?"

"See," her husband told her, "I was right to hide that money."

"OK...black market...but never mind..." agreed Kate.

Their last stop was Kraków.

Kate asked her husband to be careful with her family here. Her uncle was something big in the "Party"...a chairman...and so it would not do to insult him by asking him if he wanted any dollars.

They arrived in Kraków. What a beautiful city. Even, despite the ugly, grey communist tower blocks which made each city in Poland look so bleak.

It was lovely to see her family in Kraków. Her uncle and aunt and her two cousins welcomed them with the usual Polish hospitality. They had little in Poland, as she knew. Every item of food had to be queued for from the crack of dawn, and yet wherever they went, they were welcomed with a "banquet". Even lemon tea...lemons had been saved for months for their visit.

Her uncle asked Kate's husband if he had any dollars. He took him aside quite soon after their arrival and asked for dollars. No insult, then... no worries. Even big officials needed dollars. So, there it was then, no one was exempt from the black market. Poland only survived using this system.

The three weeks went by, and they were on their way back. Back to the border. Back to the minute checks, the minute scrutiny of documents, the long delays. They had their documents, they had their receipts, and...they had a huge crystal vase which had been given to them as a present by her family.

They arrived at the Polish border. Ahead of them was a little green Volkswagen.

The official came up to them very politely and asked to see all their documents and gave them a customs form to fill in...as if they hadn't enough paperwork.

The Volkswagen in front was being taken apart. The officials had opened up the boot, and were taking out everything that was in it. The passengers watched, as the mats, the seat covers, their luggage was taken out and searched.

Kate got out and spoke to the official.

"Sir..." they were always so polite in Poland, "I have a large crystal vase. A present. I don't know whether it should be noted on this customs form, because I didn't buy it. It is a present."

"Madam, you will have to pay customs duty on it."

"What do you mean? Customs duty? I didn't buy it...it was a present."

Kate's husband wanted to know what he was saying, and indicated the Volskwagen ahead.

"Don't argue," he muttered. "For God's sake, don't argue."

Don't argue...don't argue...? What was wrong with him? Don't argue... my foot, she thought.

"Sir, I will not pay customs duty on this vase."

"Madam, you must."

"No, I mustn't...I did not buy it. Sir, what did you expect me to say to my family...what did you expect me to say...? Don't give me this vase because I will have problems on the border...is that what you expected me to say, sir?"

"Madam, they should have known that such goods are not allowed out of the country, without paying customs duty."

"Where, sir...does it say this on this customs form? Where does it say that you cannot accept presents from your family because you will have to pay duty? Go on, please, show me on the customs form..."

"Madam, nevertheless, whatever it says..."

"No, if it doesn't say it on this form, sir...how was I to know, how was my family to know...?"

"Madam...please..."

"Well, sir...in that case...you take this vase...you take it."

"Don't argue..."her husband continued to mutter... "For God's sake don't argue."

"Madam, I cannot take this vase...you have to pay customs duty..."

"Well, I won't, so there, you have it, sir...I am not paying anything for it."

He walked away with the vase, and she got back into the car.

"Don't argue, you always argue..." Huh, she thought of Magdeburg but decided that this wasn't a good time to mention Magdeburg.

The customs official came back, and she got out of the car again.

"Madam," he was smiling wearily, "madam, please take your vase...please take yourself and your car...and go..."

"No duty, then..."she smiled.

"No duty…"

"Go on, go on…" she said to her husband, "go…go…go…we're OK, he's letting us go."

They took a last look at the Volkswagen and its passengers and all their belongings lying on the pavement, and went.

Kate came back to the prison.

"Kate," her manager said, "you didn't fill out that form I told you about. The declaration that you wouldn't get involved in any black market activities."

"I'll fill it in now," she read…"Mmmmm, no black market activities, no possible reasons for being blackmailed as a person working for the British Government…Mmmmm."

She signed it…

Pre-Release

Kate was being asked to start another new course. This was a course that would be delivered to those who were due to be released, and it was to give the prisoners a grounding about life outside and how to cope with it.

She decided that it would have two parts. One would be a Lifeskills part. The teachers would give the students a foundation in coping with relationships, and a second part which would entail managing financially.

The course would run for four weeks. The first group of students would start with Lifeskills, which would be divided into two separate courses each taking one week to complete. The first group would move into the second course in Lifeskills, whilst at the same time a second group would join them. The first group would move after two weeks to the Financial course, and stay there for two weeks, whilst group two would move to week two, and so on. In effect, after the first four weeks, there would be a new group starting each Monday, joining the remainder of the last group, of which half will have moved to the Financial course and so on.

This would mean that there would be no settled group, as in the Main Department with people coming into a well-established system in ones and twos. And so, every Monday there would be new group dynamics and the teacher would have to create some form of system in order so that he or she would stay in control. This would not be easy.

Kate decided that she would be the first one each Monday to teach the new group. The first at the cliff face, so to speak. She knew that in order for everyone to cope for the next month, she would have to show her authority within the first few minutes every Monday. If she "lost" them early on, there would be problems further down the line. No pressure on her then.

The classrooms were on the wing. The students had to be brought from a different wing and so they tended to come in as a group, and had to be settled immediately.

"Hi, everyone. Good morning to those I already know from last week, and good morning to our newcomers...This particular week I will be starting with Group Dynamics and next week, look at Anger Management."

The group looked sullen, even hostile. Good start.

"Group Dynamics. By the end of this session..." she wrote on the flipchart... "By the end of this session, we will know how dynamics work, especially within a group. We will look at group pressure, and how to avoid it...difficult, let me say...We will look at what happens to groups as the dynamics change..."

Some of them had sprawled out in their chairs. She couldn't have that.

"OK, everyone...this is a class. Before we start, let us lay down some rules which we will all respect for this week. Could someone start with a rule that might be essential for this class to run, so that everyone within it is treated with respect?"

Oh dear, they were not responding...and she had minutes...

"Maybe I should put that on the flipchart...everyone must be treated with respect..." she wrote. "Including me, gentlemen... What does that mean, though...treated with respect...?"

Pulling teeth...pulling teeth...this was going to be fun...she would start pulling out their teeth, so help her, if they were going to remain so hostile...

"Come on, someone from last week's group...what about confidentiality...? What about letting everyone have their say...what about ...?"

"I don't want to be in this class..." muttered an ugly monster of a bloke...Mr. Smart Ass. He was not really an ugly monster, but Kate was not in the mood for being kind...

"OK, so why did you come here then...hmmmm?" Keep smiling, Kate, keep smiling. Just try to remember that those in most need of this class were actually the ones who were most difficult. Big smile, Kate...

"OK, why did you, why did you come to this class?"

"Something to do... Boring, isn't it?"

"Oh, wonderful, so you are bored..." Don't lose it, Kate, she thought, don't lose it...that's what he wants...He is just scared, so he is reacting...is trying to humiliate her, so that he looks big in front of his mates...he has little self-confidence and so he's just scared...just testing...just playing a game...

"Yeah...what you going to teach us then, get on with it..." He looked around at the others and grinned maliciously. They sniggered back...Well, Kate thought...Well, so much for this morning... They would get a shock in a minute...hmmmm.

"OK, I have chosen to teach here in this prison because I like teaching adults. Polite, pleasant adults, and today, I have made a mistake, today, I am not teaching adults but little boys. Today, I am not teaching people who have the maturity to listen and learn..." Oooooh dear...

"Yeah...cos you are treating us like kids..." Mr Smart Ass...

"Oh please, please don't give me that one…please, Mr…Mr…(no, don't call him Smart Ass, Kate!)…Hudson…Mmmm. It's so boring. If I could have a pound every time I hear that pathetic excuse for rudeness, bad manners, and excuse for acting like an imbecile, I would be a very rich woman by now, and not have to come in to teach you, Mr. Hudson…" Smart Ass…

"And so, class…I wonder who thinks it was my birthday yesterday? Hmmmmm? Was I born yesterday? Mr. Hudson clearly does, and so, let's see…please pick up your things and we will go back to your wing…yes…I'm bored now…I don't want to teach you…"

They started to object. They began to apologise. Mr Hudson was not looking happy. They were promising that they would behave, that they would be pleasant and behave, and listen to her, and do whatever she said…no! NO! NO!

"Get your things and come with me."

She was already at the door and was beckoning them out.

"Come on, gentlemen…back to your wing…"

All the way down the landing they argued and promised and promised and argued, but she would not give in. Back to the wing!

The officers in the wing were surprised that their little cherubs were returning so soon.

"I'm sorry," said Kate, "Couldn't teach them, they didn't want to know."

The following week they came in very meekly…hmmmmm.

It was not always so bad. Sometimes, the group was enthusiastic and motivated.

"OK, so we have rules. We will respect each other. We will listen to each other. We will respect confidentiality. We will work together."

"And now," Kate would start the lesson, "you all on this side are Group A, and you all on this side are Group B. We're going to have a quiz."

She would enjoy teaching the enthusiastic ones. It was so interesting to point out to them how once she had divided them into two groups, the two groups became competitive, and started competing with each other for points and to win!

There were also those who would be quiet and let the other members of the group lead, and there were those who were happy to be the leaders. They were learning how a group functions, how easy it is to get molded into the group dynamics, and follow the leaders.

"Do all leaders lead well, guys? Must we always follow the leader? Why not?...Are all leaders right in what they say and do, guys? Leaders...are you always right? Do you always know the right path? You do....Oh my God, have we got leaders to beat leaders in this class?

When someone tells you what to do...do you think? What happens to your thoughts? Do you respect your thoughts? Do you give yourself time to think? Maybe we all need time to think sometimes, guys. I'm the prime example of someone who doesn't give herself time to think...yes, honestly...I'm always saying 'yes' to things I don't want to do...I know, and I'm standing here teaching *you* what to do...hah!

OK, now I'm going to do a bit of role playing...Who doesn't mind role playing? Paul? OK, I'll start with you...Whatever I say, and whatever I do, you will say no to me. You think you can...easy...hmmmm...you don't know how persuasive I can be. OK, the rest of you, watch and learn the Kate method of persuasion and let's see how long he can hold out.

Paul, last month I helped you, didn't I? I gave you that loan when you were short of cash. I was so good to you, Paul, do you remember? I didn't ask any questions, I gave you a loan, just like that. You said then that if *I* ever needed any help at all...hmmmm, you did...you would help *me*. Now, you promised that you would help me paint my hallway...Next weekend my family is coming down and I need to paint the hallway this Saturday...Is that OK? You will come to help, won't you?"

"Ummm," Paul has to say no. "No, I can't. I can't this Saturday."

"What do you mean, you can't...you said...if I wanted any help...why can't you on Saturday?"

"Ummmm, I'm busy."

"What do you mean, 'busy'? You can't be so busy that you won't help me."

"Ummmm, I've got to help my mum paint."

"Yes, but you can leave that till the following Saturday, can't you? It's really urgent. My family coming and all that...I've got to paint my hallway this Saturday."

"Ummmm, no I can't because my mum will be cross." Go on, Paul!

"Cross? Cross? Are you still scared of your mum? Are you still her little boy? Hmmm?" Kate was being mischievous. Paul was smiling. The class was egging him on...say no, say no...

"I tell you what," said Kate, "you can come in the morning to help me paint my hallway...then you can go and help your mum. How about that? That's fair."

"OK", said Paul, "OK, I'll come in the morning."

"No, don't give in, I'm being unreasonable. I can't ask you to drop everything...don't tell me that I am unreasonable, keep from attacking me personally, but tell me that what I'm asking is a little unreasonable, and you need time...time to think...don't let me get you. Go on, try it. Ask me for time...go on, go on..."

"Miss, can I have time to think about it? It feels a bit unreasonable to have to paint your hallway at such short notice, but I'll think about it."

"Good, Paul...Once you've had time, you can tell me more assertively that you cannot paint my hallway. Well done, and thank you.

Does anyone else want to have a go? Now you all want to take me on...good, good. Stay polite, stay calm, but don't let me get my own way by forcing you on a guilt trip."

So mostly, Kate thoroughly enjoyed her Monday morning. But come Sunday evening, she dreaded the morning. Would it be a march down the wing, or an enjoyable class?

The Pre-Release course developed and developed. Eventually, it became an accredited Lifeskills course and even officers took part in the presentation. Small things grow...

Loneliness

"Hi Greg, did you want to see me?" Kate was packing away her things after the lesson. Greg was one of her favourite students. He was cheeky but nice.

"Yes, Kate, I do." He hesitated. "You know how I feel about you, of course?"

"No, what? How do you feel...no, don't say it, please..." Oh no! This was all she needed.

"And I know that you feel the same."

What?

"I don't feel the same. Well, if ..." What was she going to do now?

"You'd better go, Greg, the officer's waiting."

She sat down with her head in her hands. Of course, this was one of the concerns of working in the prison. The students became attached. The teachers were kind, and the students responded with feelings. These were true feelings of course, but could not possibly be love, as they imagined. They knew their teachers professionally only, not personally, and they often mistook the warmth, affection, attachment that they felt to these women who "cared" for them, for love. After all, everyone was fed a diet of love songs, love films, love poems, from time immemorial, and it was so easy when you had no outlet for your feelings to mistake them for romantic "love".

But what was she going to do now? She couldn't continue teaching Greg. He would have to come off her classes, but that would be such a pity, because he was doing so well.

For the time being, she would wait and see. He was out in a few weeks anyway.

The next class with Greg was awkward.

"Today, we're going to do communication, guys. By the end of this session, you will know how to communicate assertively and listen, really listen to what others say..." She couldn't help but glance at Greg. He was smiling at her knowingly. Knowingly! Why did he have to be annoying? She was now really annoyed with him. How could he just assume, just assume that she had some romantic feelings for him? He was making her feel awkward, and she needed to concentrate on her class.

"OK, class...I'm standing on the landing, hoping that my Education Manager will come by. She's always so busy and I need to have a word with her. It's very important...Here she comes...H...h...hullo, h...h...hullo," Kate whispers, "c..c..can I have a quick w...w...w...word with you?...She's gone...she's gone, guys! She took no notice of me at all, and disappeared. Why didn't she take any notice of me? Hmmm?"

"I didn't get her attention...good, John, you're right. OK, I'll get her attention this time..."

"Here she comes, guys...hey you...I want to speak to you and you're always busy..!" Kate bellows. "She's gone again, guys. What the hell?" The class is laughing. "I don't know why you're laughing. I need to speak to her urgently, I got her attention and she buggered off."

"OK....you think something more in between will do the trick? Or shall I just try to trip her up...? No, you're right...she wouldn't listen to me then...ever!"

"Hullo, Mary...I can see you're busy, but I need to see you urgently...so...? She's stopped guys...she's heard me...Yehhhh! What did I do right? I didn't whisper, and I didn't bellow, I think that was a good start...what else?"

She writes their suggestions on the white board, and glances at Greg. He's still looking smug, and smiling knowingly.

Her class in communication continues.

She tells them about listening skills, about real listening skills.

They're going to play a game. A "communicating effectively and listening properly" game.

"OK, John, I will give Mark a piece of paper with a drawing on it. You will go outside, John, so that you don't see the drawing. You, Mark, have to communicate the drawing to John at the whiteboard. He has to listen to your precise...hmmm...precise Mark, instructions, ask for clarification if necessary and draw on the board. At the end of the exercise, John and Mark's drawings will match, hopefully."

Everyone enjoys games. The class enjoys this one. Everyone helps Mark, so that instructions come from all sides. Poor John. At times he is shouted down because he draws the wrong line, the wrong circle. It's too small...it's too big...that doesn't look like a cloud...

Kate laughs with them. She is enjoying the game and also shouting instructions to John.

They have more turns at the board and at instructing. Then discuss what they have learnt from the lesson.

The class ends, and Kate asks Greg to stay behind.

"Greg, you've made it so awkward for me. Please, please..."

"But Kate, you know you feel the same. You keep looking at me, I know you do."

"I do, but that's because I don't know what to do. I really should have you off the class. I don't feel anything towards you except the great respect I give all my students, honestly, you have to believe me."

"Kate, don't be silly, you look at me more than at the others, you know you do."

"You have to go…"

At the beginning of the next lesson with that class, she had to make a decision.

"Guys…this is very difficult for me…please forgive me, Greg….I need to talk to the class."

Greg was looking anxious. She was horrified at what she was about to do, but she saw no other way.

"Greg has indicated to me that he thinks that I have special feelings for him," she stuttered, "he has told me that I look at him more than I do at the rest of you, and therefore …"

There was utter silence.

"I would like to use today's lesson to look at the feelings of being in a prison, an institution like this. I would like us all to work together and examine what being in an institution like this makes us feel, you know what I mean…"

She knew that she wasn't being too clear. She was looking at Greg now.

"Greg, I'm so sorry. I'm so sorry. I do not wish to humiliate you, and I know I have. It's just that as this is a Lifeskills class, I think the class together can help here. And we can get it sorted somehow."

There was still a silence. Greg was looking down. He'd put his elbow on his lap and was holding his head in his hand.

"She doesn't look at you any more than the rest of us, mate." Good old Simon, trying to ease the situation. "Honest, she doesn't".

Another silence.

This time Greg broke the silence. "She does, Simon, she does, you don't know...you don't watch her like I do." He was looking at all of them accusingly, and they looked back sympathetically.

"You're just lonely," John said, "like the rest of us. We're lonely in this place."

"John's right. We're so f.... lonely, and then we latch on to people...you know what I mean, Greg mate," Simon again.

"We latch on to people to try to take away that empty feeling," Mark agreed. "If someone can take away that empty feeling, you can have something to look forward to, yeah...it's true..."

"I know what lonely is." Greg again, "I know what lonely is, and you don't have to preach to me, any of you. Kate has feelings for me, and she can't get away with saying she doesn't."

"She doesn't mate, she doesn't," even quiet Reg joined in, "she feels for you like she does the rest of us. She likes you but it's like she likes a friend, like she likes all of us, like she wants to help us. You know that's true. Listen to us."

Kate didn't say anything, because there wasn't much she could say. They were so right, and Greg would listen to them more than to her.

"Listen," this time Eamonn spoke, "listen, don't sit alone in your cell, don't think and think and think, until you're going stupid, just come and talk to us. You're out soon. We can be there for you."

At the end of the lesson, Greg went out first.

"Don't you worry, Miss, we'll take care of him." They crowded round her. "Don't worry, he'll be OK."

Greg didn't come to the next lesson, and she had worried. She was worried.

"He's OK, really," they assured her.

What could she really do? If she told anyone else but them, Greg would be off her class and in another prison within days. Maybe that would have been better, but it felt like a punishment. He did not deserve punishment. What for? For being lonely?

Greg came to the next lesson, and he seemed fine. He joined in and was as cheeky as he had always been. Thank God, she thought. It was going to be OK.

Then his last lesson. He asked if he could speak to her at the end.

"Of course." Actually, she was dreading what he was going to say.

"Kate, I've got a job. I'm going to be DJ-ing in a club."

"That's brilliant, brilliant. Good luck."

"I've written the address on this piece of paper. You can come to see me. You can come to the club."

"I can't, Greg. I'm not allowed to see you."

"Please, Kate, please come." He started to cry.

"Greg, please believe me, trust me," she was stumbling again, "as soon as you walk out of that gate, you will not want to look back. I promise, I promise. You won't want any reminders of this place. Honestly, trust me. You will walk out of the gate, and you will want to forget about this place, my classes, and me."

"No, I won't Kate, I won't."

He would, she knew he would. Once in that outside world with all its distractions, all its joys and sorrows, its responsibilities and hardships, he would forget her.

"So, good luck, my dear student," she said, "good luck. Play that music loudly. Enjoy!!!"

"Good-bye, Kate."

"Good-bye."

PART TWO

THE EDUCATION MANAGER

Krysia Martin

Education Manager

The Education Manager had gone. The staff were having a drink together, and worrying about who would replace her. For the time being the Deputy Manager would be Acting Manager, but then who? He didn't want the job.

Prison Education had been privatised, which meant that they, as a staff, were now contracted to a new employer every five years, whilst continuing to work in the prison. In effect, this meant that their employer had little real power in the prison, whilst the prison would see them as contracted staff and would not feel too concerned about them either. Betwixt and between. Eventually, funding would go to the Learning and Skills Council, which was better, because at least someone was looking at Prison Education directly and how to improve it, rather than how much money they could make from it, but again if you were contracted to a poor employer, neither the prison nor the Learning and Skills Council could help.

In the pub one of the members of staff stood up.

"I want to say something, everyone. Kate, we the staff have thought and thought and thought about this and we think you should go for the job."

Kate looked horrified. Anyone with an ounce of common sense and self-preservation would not want the Education Manager's job. Basically, it required a sacrificial lamb, who would take the rough from both the prison and the contractor, and there was no smooth. It required someone who would "protect" the staff, who had, by now, grown to fifty odd; someone who could "protect" the ethos of the department, and the attitude to the students; someone who could work with the contractor and the prison; a painter and decorator, carpenter, cleaner, magician; data inputter; analyst; Excel whizzkid and someone who could manage and organise a department, with too much or too little interference. Not much pressure there, then.

The staff implored; if they got someone who was difficult, someone with whom they couldn't work, someone who was abrasive and belligerent, they would all suffer, including Kate.

Kate said she'd think about it. She thought about it and was not convinced. She thought and thought a little more. Eventually, she said she would.

So she took on the job.

An Education Manager.

A Manager of a Prison Education Department and martyr.

Trouble

As they had no officers in the Education Department, they policed themselves, or rather, they policed themselves, and if something went badly wrong, they could ring the alarm bell and have the officers there to help within minutes, or call Kate, the Education Manager.

In a prison, you would expect trouble all the time, and it's true, sometimes the alarm bell would go off several times a day in the wings, however, in the Education Department, apart from the odd mistake, the bell was rarely rung. In fact, it was so rare, that it had probably been rung for real twice in the last twenty years. Prisoners coming into Education were coming into an established routine, which they usually accepted and made no trouble about. The teachers, too, were experienced and generally were perfectly able to control a class.

The problem was that more and more prisoners had some sort of mental health issue and it was difficult to anticipate how they would respond, which could cause problems.

Jamie was a student in the Art class. He was autistic, could not read or write, but painted the most intricate art work. The problem was that he would never actually finish a painting. Well, that was not quite true; the painting appeared finished to all intents and purposes, but Jamie would say it was not finished, because somehow in his eyes, the "unfinished" paintings were still his, whereas "finished" paintings were out of his hands. So he would continue finishing his paintings, with a dab of paint here and a dab of paint there, a line…a curve…for a very long time. He was gradually gathering canvases of "unfinished" art work, some of it hardly started, which was not helpful when the Art Department did not have canvases to waste.

He was a model student otherwise, worked hard, and got on well with the others.

Then one day, Kate, whose office was some way from the department, had a phone call to say there was trouble in the Art Room. She tried to walk as quickly as she could (you are only allowed to run in the prison in an emergency) to the department, and when she unlocked the gate into Education, Jamie was standing there.

"Miss, Miss," he tried to speak to her...

"Not now, Jamie, there's trouble in Art..."

"I know, I know. I am the trouble, Miss..."

"Don't be silly, Jamie, and get back to your classroom."

However, when she went into the Art Room the teacher showed her a canvas which had been ripped apart with a Stanley knife. He told her that Jamie had just painted a sky on the canvas, and was "finishing off" his other work, insisting that this canvas was his. The teacher had taken the canvas away to give to someone else. Jamie had slashed it with a Stanley knife.

Kate went out to Jamie.

"What happened to you?" she asked, "Why on earth did you destroy our precious Art stuff?"

"It was mine, Miss, and so it shouldn't be given to someone else."

"But you'd barely started on it, and you've already got, how many canvases on the go...?"

"Yes, but those other ones are nearly finished and then I can start on this one..."

"Jamie, that was terrible, what you did. The only good thing that I can say is that you attacked an object and not a person. However, this is absolutely appalling and you will be suspended for this for a month. In fact, I'm going to ask the teacher if you should be taken off the class altogether."

"But Miss, it was mine, my canvas…he had no right…"

"It was not your canvas, it belongs to the department, and I am extremely angry with you. I am going to take you back to your cell, and I will let you know by tomorrow what we intend to do with you."

"Miss, Miss…"

"No, you are lucky that I don't put you on report, so help me…. Now back with me to your cell."

What do you do when someone doesn't really understand the reasons for his suspension?

Kate had a word with the Art Teacher. It was unfair for him to have Jamie in his class, when Jamie could be so unpredictable. She decided to phone the Day Care Centre in the hospital and have a word with the Manager, asking if Jamie could be transferred to the Art classes there. They had officers in the hospital and trained psychiatric help, so Jamie would be better off there. Before he could get there however, he was transferred to another prison.

Kate was in the department when she heard an altercation outside in the corridor. A teacher was talking quietly to a student, who appeared very angry and unresponsive. Kate moved towards them:

"Do you think that it might be a good idea if you go back to your cell for a while, Freddie? You seem to be very upset."

"OK," he muttered. Again, he was one of their "specials" and normally worked well. He walked calmly into the classroom, picked up his books and suddenly turned, screamed something and began to throw the books everywhere.

"OK, OK, Freddie. It's OK." Both Kate and the teacher began to move towards him, telling the others to remain calm. Freddie began to sob loudly, and turned to a Peer Support, Stan, who happened to be in the room,

"Help me, help me..." he implored Stan. Stan put his arms round Freddie, and began to move with him out of the classroom. Kate walked beside them.

"It's OK, Freddie, no one is going to hurt you. No one is going to hurt you," she kept repeating, but she could see that he was terrified.

Outside in the corridor, Freddie broke away and ran towards the gates. He was sobbing and screaming. Stan was doing his best to calm him, and Kate went to the alarm bell. There was nothing she could do any longer.

One last try...

"Freddie," she shouted, as she moved her hand nearer and nearer to the bell push. "Freddie, I am going to ring this alarm bell, unless you calm down... Look, my hand is getting closer..."

He went quiet and collapsed onto Stan's shoulder.

"All right, all right. I'm going to take you to the wing now...You're all right. Don't worry," she told him.

Six weeks later, Freddie bit off an officer's finger.

The ESOL (English for Speakers of Other Languages) Co-ordinator rang Kate in her office, to say that one of his students had something urgent to ask her.

"Be down in a sec."

Mr Laseki was anxious that his birth date on the prison computer was wrong, and he wanted to ask Kate, should he give that birth date in court or his real one.

"Oh, real one, of course. You will be swearing to tell the whole truth in court. But where did you say you saw your birth date on a computer?" He was evasive, and she wondered if it was true. However, she left it like that.

The Co-ordinator followed her:

"You see, he says that he is God..."

"God?"

"Yes, so actually what he's telling you is, that he has no birth date..."

"OK, OK." A tricky one, this. Kate had just completed a course in Personality Disorders. She couldn't diagnose, of course, because she was not a Psychiatrist, but she tried to remember what she had been taught about delusional behaviour.

"OK. I will try to get him moved to the Daycare classes."

"Ummm, slight problem," said the Co-ordinator. "He absolutely refuses to go to the hospital, even for days."

"Oh God, we can't have him here. If anyone argues that he isn't God, he's likely to hit the roof, and then we have a problem."

Kate rang the Psychiatric nurse who was very sympathetic, but said that he would be OK, unless someone argued with him. So far, so much Kate knew already.

"OK, what do you want to do with him?" she asked the Co-ordinator. "It would be cruel to take him off classes."

"Well, he's no trouble, and he doesn't tell everyone that he is God, so maybe we can hold on to him, and see how it goes."

"But tell the teachers to hit that alarm bell immediately, if they suspect that there is going to be a problem. No hesitation," Kate advised. "And tell them never to argue with him about being God. He can be God if he wants to be."

He was no trouble, and worked in the classroom every day very quietly and conscientiously, until he was moved to another prison.

One morning, Kate had a phone call from an administrator. There was trouble in the Art class again.

Oh no, the Art class was usually so well behaved.

Kate hurried to the department, and walked into the Art class. About ten hefty prisoners were sitting in there painting. As she walked in, she could *smell* the hostility. There was an uneasy silence, except for the radio which was playing music loudly.

She walked carefully to the radio and switched it off.

"Now you know that there is to be no music in a classroom, guys," she said. The teacher moved out of the room, probably having had enough by now.

"Who says?" - a belligerent voice from the other side of the room.

"The Learner Forum says. The Learner Forum agreed at one of the first meetings that there would be no music in any classroom," she said firmly. "You can read the decisions and rules of the Learner Forum outside," she added.

"Who's the Learner Forum?" Belligerent again.

"Are you new?" she asked, "If so, let me tell you, that the Learner Forum is a group of students, representing all of you, which meets once every two months."

"So, who are they to decide anything?" another belligerent voice.

"We agreed that they would have a say about the rules and regulations in the Education Department." She was getting impatient with this now.

"Who are *we*?" Belligerent One.

"The Learner Forum...Guys, this is stupid, I'm not going to spend the rest of my morning explaining things to you that you don't want to hear. Basically, if you come to Education, you will abide by the rules, as you signed on your first day here...This is your first day...? OK...You will be signing a contract to say that you will...

"No, we ain't," Belligerent One or Two, she couldn't really distinguish between them.

"Well then, you come off Education, so please go to the office now, you and you..." pointing at both Belligerents.

"No!"

OK, she was going to have a problem.

"I am the Education Manager, and when I say go to the office, you will go to the office."

The Belligerents began to mutter something, which sounded like bitch.

"Did you just call me a bitch?" she said. "Go to the office...."

"He didn't call you a bitch," other Belligerent.

"I never called you bitch," first Belligerent, "did I call her a bitch?" This, to the class, who had lowered their heads and were trying not to get involved.

"Do not involve the class, just go to the office now." Her voice was still calm, although it was gradually getting firmer and louder.

"He never called you bitch, and we're not going to the office, make us..."

Well, here was a problem, no exaggeration. If she let them get away with it, she would not have respect as an Education Manager, but if she pursued this, there could be real trouble. If she rang the alarm bell, she'd win, but only with the help of the officers, which would also lose her respect. A dilemma. Could she cope with this one? She needed to show that she had authority. She needed to show that the staff in the Education Department were not weak and born yesterday. She needed to enforce her authority or it would be questioned again, and she could not afford to have it questioned or the department would not be as safe as it was now.

She could hear that the students from the other classes had gathered in the corridor to see what was going on. Great. She and the two Belligerents had an audience, and they would not want to lose face. If she could just get them into the office.

They were both shouting now: they were not going to be treated like children; they were not going to be treated like idiots; they were not going to the office; who did she think she was....etc etc.

Kate put her head down, and became quiet. After several seconds, so did they. There was silence in the room. No one moved a muscle. What was going to happen now?

Slowly, slowly, as slowly and emphatically as she could, she began to walk towards the teacher's desk, to the front of the class. There was complete silence, and you could only hear her footsteps. She knew she was really burning her boats as the teacher's desk was further from the alarm bell, and if trouble erupted, she was not going to be able to get to that alarm bell as easily.

When she reached the teacher's desk, she stopped. Again, as slowly as she could, she turned to face the class. She waited for a few more seconds, then raised her hand into the air, and with all her might, slammed it down on the desk. Hard! So hard, that she felt her hand burn. The sound was like a gunshot.

"If I tell you to go to the office, you go to the office. NOW!" she shouted.

They got up immediately and pushed their way to the door into the corridor. She didn't know why it had worked, except that it had. Maybe because normally she spoke pleasantly and respectfully to the students, and this Kate was scary, authoritarian, loud, angry. Whatever. She had got them out of the classroom.

She winked at the rest of the class and followed the Belligerents.

In the office, she asked them to give their names to the administrator, and their numbers, and told the administrator to take them off all classes immediately. Then she asked one of the teachers to take Belligerent Two back to his cell, whilst she told Belligerent One that she would accompany him back to his.

She was still very angry, and walked very purposefully down the wing, with the offending student.

"I never called you bitch, Miss." Now away from the others, he had lost his nerve somewhat, and was speaking to her pleasantly again.

"Do you know about Karma?" she asked. She knew that this was really mischievous, but she was so angry. "If you really didn't call me bitch then all will be well, but if you did, someone will do the same to you, today. Someone will do something unpleasant and unkind to you, but then will lie and say he didn't."

Oh my, how cruel. He deserved it, she reasoned to herself.

He thought for a while:

"I didn't call you a bitch, Miss, I just said that you were acting like a bitch. Will that stop the Karma?"

"Who knows? Maybe it will, maybe it won't. I don't know with Karma....Anyway here is your wing...I will just tell the officer that I've brought you back, and fill in your contract, that you are off Education. I hope it was worth having the radio on, hmmmmm..."

As she went back to the Education Department, her legs began to shake. In height, she had just come up to the two offenders' shoulders, but she had had to stand her ground and not be afraid to insist on the rules being followed. But what if they had...? It would never happen, would it? But there was always a first time...She had never been afraid to face the troublemakers, in fact, her staff thought that she had no fear. Well, she didn't at the time, but afterwards when her legs turned to jelly, and she began to think over what could have happened...then....

In the department, some of the students were still in the corridor, to see if she was all right...

"Well I live to see another day..." she called out more cheerfully than she felt.

"So, back to your classrooms, everyone."

No one argued.

Adult Learners' Week

As they collapse into any chair that is available, the teachers are still in a state of absolute exhaustion, but buzzing with the excitement of the week. It has been Adult Learners Week.

Plans have been afoot for weeks. Meetings about the "Theme", the content, the organisation, the responsibilities and meetings about meetings have been happening more and more frequently, and Luke, in charge of the "Week", has been rallying staff, trying to fit the plans into the prison regime, get permission for this, permission for that, count, allocate, collect resources, organise, organise and organise. His diplomatic skills are brought to bear as he tries to juggle a flexible plan which will fit into the fixed, immovable prison regime. He will need to observe security first and foremost, so he will need to reassure the Security Department and keep them informed. He will have to encourage teachers who do not like change and curtail those whose plans are too ambitious. He will need to reassure the Heads of the prison departments. He will need to reassure in particular, the Principal Officer in charge of the regime, Oscar 1. He will need to reassure the Education Manager that nothing should go wrong and ensure that the Education Department doesn't find itself in the middle of some riot or some huge embarrassment. He will need to have every eventuality covered, and every move accounted for…in a prison!

The theme is to be based loosely on diversity, "Our Culture". Five classrooms are to be used. Classroom One will have tasters for the Dyslexia Support Course, alternating with Meditation, and "educational" games, such as Call My Bluff, (dictionary practice), a scrabble tournament and quiz tournaments. Classroom Two, the Art class will have painting around the "Our Culture" theme. Classroom Three will have tasters in Music Technology, Art Technology and a Maths

Quiz Tournament. Classroom Four will concentrate on Creative Writing around the theme, and Classroom Five will have tasters in computing. Prisoners will choose which class they want to attend, and on a first chosen, first served basis, will be allocated to the various classrooms for the week.

Only the week is very popular, and everyone and his cell mate wants to attend. So from the start, approximately eighty prisoners apply. That has to be the limit, however, eighty applications mean eighty names on an unlocking list which means finding eighty locations and allocating them to their chosen classes on the prison database. It means putting the names of those attending on the classroom doors, so that everyone knows where they should be. It means checking in those who are due to be attending, and counting the figures correctly, so that they tally with the wing figures. It also means teachers escorting students to their allocated classrooms, and making sure that they stay there; that they are engaged immediately, and that therefore they do not wander unnecessarily in the department corridor. Large numbers of prisoners, disengaged...doesn't bear thinking about.

Monday, Day One. There are two Education sites: in G Wing and E Wing. It has been decided that everything will happen on E Wing and so G Wing is not going to be used. However, not all teachers have keys, so it is agreed that teachers will arrive at their usual teaching site and if necessary be escorted to E Wing for the Learners Week.

On Monday, Luke, Derek, the Deputy Education Manager, and Kate, arrive at 7.45 in G Wing. The teachers too, have been asked to come earlier, so that they are ready for the onslaught.

The Managers sit down for a calm cup of coffee, while Luke rushes over to prepare E Wing.

Then the Managers wait... and wait. And wait. 8 o'clock comes and it is like the Marie Celeste. No one has arrived. 8.05...all quiet...8.10...no teachers...and there are only three of them so far, to manage eighty prisoners at 8.30. Hmmmmm.

Kate decides that they must have all gone straight to E Wing, so she rings Luke over there...No one there either...The Marie Celeste...not a soul. Only Luke.

Kate goes across to E Wing. Luke and she check that all is ready for the prisoners to arrive. The classrooms are ready. The names are on the doors. All is prepared, but there are no teachers.

Derek and she keep phoning each other, which doesn't help any, but does stop them from having nothing to do but worrying more.

8.15 comes and goes...where on earth are the teachers? The prison is already unlocking the eighty.

8.20...A teacher, Nick, arrives in G Wing. They are doing a big search at the main gate, he tells them, and all the teachers are trapped there.

Nick has keys so he hurries over to E Wing. There are three there now, to take care of eighty students... Derek must wait for any teachers without keys to arrive.

8.25...The officers ask Kate if she is ready to receive the prisoners, who are about to arrive. If she doesn't take them, they will be milling around the wing, and if she takes them, they will be milling around the Education Department. What to do?

She asks Nick and Luke to go into Classroom One, and she will send all the prisoners into them. All eighty? Hope it doesn't come to that. They don't bat an eye. They are experienced teachers. However... how long can they hold the prisoners before they erupt? It's like battle stations.

8.30...The prisoners start arriving...Kate welcomes them at the Education Gate, and begins a Litany...

"Guys, terribly sorry...teachers held up at the main gate...can you go into this classroom...yes, that's right...yes, Nick and Luke are in there...don't worry...the teachers will be here soon..."

The Litany begins to sound desperate by 8.35:

"Guys...terribly sorry...teachers held...go into classroom...is there room? That's right...thank you, thank you...that's right...everything is going wrong, but don't worry...Nick, Luke are you OK?"

The teachers are coming! Thank God, the teachers are coming. Walking as fast as they can (they cannot run in the prison) up the landing...Thank you God, thank you.

"OK," Kate, so relieved... "OK, guys, the teachers are here...Teachers go and prepare the other classrooms...thank you, thank you."

There are about twenty prisoners squashed into Classroom One by now. All laughing and joking, but thankfully, not getting too boisterous, and no one is being difficult.

"Thank you, thank you for your patience," calls out Kate. "Classroom Two and Three are ready to go..."

"All those for the Maths Quiz, that's..." she reels out the names... "go now, to classroom Three...No, no, no...I haven't called your name out yet...huh..." there is always one.

Gradually they are all transferred into the correct classes and Kate can do the count.

"Now, don't move from your rooms, or else...got to do the count, and it had better be right..."

Miraculously, it all adds up. The numbers from her list add up to the numbers in the classrooms, and what is more, her teachers have already started, and the classrooms are beginning to come to order. Ten minutes later, it is so quiet in the corridor that no one would guess that there are eighty students in the department, together with about fifteen teachers. Result!

The numbers are phoned into the Centre, and Kate, Derek, Luke and Nick collapse in the staff room, laughing hysterically.

There are no more problems on Monday.

Tuesday...everyone who was in the Creative Writing class has now got a story to finish, but they are not on the same lists as they were on Monday and therefore not necessarily in the same classrooms. Of course they are anxious to go to their original class, to finish their work. But what to do with the students who are due to be in that classroom on Tuesday? Luke hadn't envisaged that Creative Writing would be so popular.

Luke and Kate keep smiling and smiling, and the teachers in the classroom are smiling and smiling. The Creative Writing class is heaving with students, but it is vital not to become harassed and impatient, or the students will pick up the vibes, and become harassed and impatient too. Harassed and impatient prisoners...

"Yes, OK, yes, you can go back in there...OK, yes, I know you are supposed to be in there but can you go to Classroom

One and the Scrabble and the Call My Bluff instead...yes, yes, yes, yes..."

Eventually...Sorted...Everyone is in a classroom. How, only God knows. But, again, some of those who had been transferred to Call my Bluff, can't read...some can't speak English...some are therefore now being transferred to the computing tasters, and looking anxious, as one does when faced with a computer for the first time. Art is very full, so no one else can be transferred in there....and as for the Maths Quiz, even Kate blanches at the formulae displayed on the whiteboard.

They sort out the last stragglers and Kate decides to see what is going on in each room.

In Class One, the bluffers are so good that it is impossible to tell who is telling the truth. Hopefully, no one from the Ministry will get to hear that they are teaching their students to lie. One teacher is playing Scrabble with a special needs student...bless her...he is so proud of himself because he seems to be winning.

"I'm beating Miss, Miss...I'm beating Miss."

There is a group around another Scrabble board, with the Champ...not been beaten throughout Monday. He is now challenging anyone to beat him. Kate laughs as he attempts to introduce extraordinary words, and there is an outcry, whilst the "judge" checks the dictionary. He insists that his words are not found in that particular dictionary as it is an old dictionary...hmmmm. The class is not convinced either, and he has to find another word.

There is an ESOL (English for Speakers of Other Languages) group doing a picture quiz in another corner. Here the teacher is explaining the pictures, which illustrate English customs - Morris Men dancing takes a while to explain, with the teacher demonstrating. Kate isn't absolutely sure if the students really know what it is about, but they seem to nod, as if they do, smiling hesitantly…probably because they are wondering why their usually sober teacher is jumping around pretending to hit things in the air…theirs not to wonder why…

She goes into Classroom Two. Ah, here is Culture and Diversity in full flow. Groups of students are painting representations of their culture. She walks over to a very noisy group of Poles, who have painted several symbols on their paper…The White Eagle, the white and red flag, a cross…but what is this woman?…Polish women are very beautiful they tell her, so they have to be in the picture, because they too symbolise Poland. "And what on earth is this aeroplane doing here?" she asks.

"It is a spitfire, Miss Kate…it is with this aeroplane that we, Poles, won the war for the British and the other Europeans."

In Classroom Three, there are clearly groups of Maths enthusiasts, who are busy conferring quietly, so as not to be overheard by other groups of competitors. Intensity and competition seem to pulsate in the air. She stares for a moment at the whiteboard…If three…are put into five…and six…..are introduced to seven…then what does three thousand million of those seven come to…if they are all the same height?…Well, that's what the question seems to be. It's like a cryptic clue in a crossword…She has no idea what it means…but the groups are conferring knowingly, and arguing about the answer…Answer? Kate doesn't stay in that room for long.

She moves over to the Creative Writing. Students are sitting, writing around a central table with teachers beside them, helping. She walks round and some of the students aren't even aware of her presence.

"What are you writing?" she asks one ESOL student.

"Miss, it is about when people come and kill my family...My mother, she die, in front of me," he tells her quietly.

The teacher beside him looks up.

"Kate, you must read this when he has finished. Heartbreaking, God, heartbreaking."

Another student seems to be writing about a wedding feast in his country, and telling the teacher enthusiastically what he is writing. Kate determines to come back after the class, to see what they have written. How interesting is each life.

Finally, she walks into the computer class. The anxious students are now looking somehow triumphant. They have managed to do something on the computer without it taking off, deleting, crashing or whatever else they thought it would do. Some are typing out their stories from the day before, some are discovering colour and font, some are even producing a poster about their culture, which they will print onto T-shirts in the Art class.

Wednesday and Thursday come and go without too many problems.

Finally, Friday morning. All are gathered in the Sports Hall upstairs above the Education Department. Their paintings, writing, posters, T-shirts and certificates for winning are all displayed around the hall, but everyone is sitting in the centre of the room, with the teachers gathered round the walls.

Now, some of the poems are read, as are some of the stories. Some play what they have composed in the Music Technology class. All contributions are greeted with enthusiastic cheering and all the winners come up to collect their certificates and prizes shyly.

Visitors have arrived from colleges and are taken around and shown what has been achieved.

"In one week...." says Kate to anyone who will listen, "in one week...."

No one mentions Monday morning, and no one would guess that anything had gone wrong. No one, except those who work in a prison, would know how much effort, patience and energy has been used during this week.

And so on Friday afternoon, the teachers collapse into any chair that is available. Exhausted!

Security calling!

All the tools anywhere in the prison are locked in a "shadow board". This is a cupboard with outlines of tools painted on the back, so that you can see immediately whether a tool is in its place or...missing. In the Education Department, these tools are checked at the start of every lesson, given out carefully, with a tally to notify who has the tool, and then checked at the end of the classes.

They are unable to use any other tools. This is particularly difficult, as they cannot use scissors with which to cut paper, no screwdrivers, no knives(!), no blue tac, because blue tac can be used to take casts of keys and to block up key holes, even chewing gum, for the same reason. Food is eaten with plastic knives and forks, and coffee and tea kept in plastic containers.

Kate had stayed late. It was 8.00 in the evening. She was about to go home, so she checked the scissors which were locked in a box, in a drawer of which the key was locked in a key cabinet. Although they were extremely careful with these scissors, they were not being kept in a shadow board, and they knew that they should not keep the scissors in a drawer. If Security found out, there would be trouble.

Kate checked for the scissors. They were not there.

She checked the whole drawer again...They were not there.

She began to check the desk, desperately to start with, then more carefully as there seemed to be no sign of the scissors. She began searching the whole room. They were not there or there, or there.

When had she seen them last? Had she checked the drawer before she went home last night? Of course, she had. She did it as a matter of course every evening before she went home. She would check that the scissors were in their box, in the drawer. She would lock the drawer carefully, she would hang the key in the little key cabinet, then put the key cabinet key on a little hook beside the drawer.

But had she done this last night? She began to doubt herself.

Come on...what was she doing last night? She had finished her work on the computer, then she had gone to lock up the classrooms, then she would have checked the scissors, locked them away, and put away the key...as she did every evening.

Oh God, had she done this last night? Or had she forgotten?

She started turning the department over. She emptied every bin. She started checking all the drawers. No scissors...no scissors...no scissors...

Of course, they could be anywhere in the prison by now...Had any of the students been in the office? They were not allowed to come in, but maybe somebody had crept in...but if the office was empty, it was always locked...Where were the scissors?

Then Kate's imagination began to go wild...they were probably in someone's back by now. Someone was probably lying in the prison, with scissors in his back.

There was no way out. It was nearly 9.00 by now. She had better report the loss of the scissors. There would be trouble...oh my, there would be trouble...

She went upstairs to the Centre to see Oscar 1, the Principal Officer in charge that evening.

"Ummm, I've...we've lost our scissors in the department..." she murmured. "Yes, I've searched the place...no, they were not on a shadow board...no, I don't know when they were used last...no, it must have been today because I always check them last thing at night...who is the Governor on duty? Nooooo...!"

The Security Governor was on duty...Not only was he fierce, but he *was* the Security Governor, and they were holding scissors in their drawer, albeit safely as far as they were concerned, but against the prison rules....

Yes, she would go back to the department and wait for the Governor there.

He came down with Oscar 1 almost immediately...

He didn't speak. She gabbled, but he didn't say a word...

"You see, this is where we...and this is where...and I've looked...."

He followed her around, but did not speak.

"Please, Governor, you can kill me if you like, but find those scissors...they might be in someone's back by now..." The look he gave her now...You do your job. I'll do mine, it seemed to say.

"Sorry, sorry," she kept pleading. "Here is a list of all those prisoners who were in the department today...with their locations..."

The Governor gave the list to Oscar 1...

Please let him say something...please, thought Kate.

"OK, were those scissors on a shadow board?" he finally spoke. "No? Why not?...In a drawer?...You kept them in a drawer?...You thought that would be OK?...Why did you not put them on a shadow board?...You thought they would be safe in the drawer?....They weren't safe, were they?...Because they have disappeared...And now we have some missing scissors somewhere in the prison..."

Oh dear, he was saying something, but it was not good... He was supposed to be reassuring her that all would be well...hmmmm...The department had been holding scissors in a drawer against the rules, and now she was for it...

"Have you searched in the department?...Everywhere?...Everywhere?...Are you certain?"

No, of course she was not certain, but she was trying to bluff it out somehow...

"I can't think where they can be. All the teachers, always put them back..." she sounded lame even to herself. If they always put them back....

"Well, you can go home now, but I'll see you in the morning," he said. Not much reassurance there, then. What did she expect?

She went home. She could not sleep. She hardly slept a wink.

Security did not hesitate. If you broke the rules of the prison, you could put your case, if you had one, before a Governor, and then if he or she decided, you would be escorted out, immediately. You would not even be allowed to get your things. You would wait at the gate for someone, usually the Manager, to bring your things to you, outside the gate. You were then not allowed back to the prison, ever...and not in any other prison either...Kate had had to do this for at least four of her teachers.

Her Art teacher had been working on an Embroidery Project in the Workshop which embroidered names on T-shirts. These T-shirts were those used by various "supports". For example, the Education Supports had red T-shirts with

EDUCATION SUPPORT embroidered on the back, Race Relations had blue ones, Day Care had green ones and so on. They also embroidered work for other prisons, such as logos, etc.

Janet, the Art teacher, had been taking photographs of the designs for the project, so that they could be incorporated into the Embroidery Machine, and used as evidence in Art accreditations.

She had taken her eye off the ball for a moment, left the camera on a table, a prisoner had picked it up, took a photo of a fellow prisoner, and the photo was found by an officer. On a Friday afternoon.

Kate was interviewed immediately. She knew that there was absolutely no excuse, nothing she could say, nothing that would defend Janet.

Janet was to be interviewed when she came in on Monday morning.

Kate tried and tried to ring her throughout the weekend. She could do nothing but warn her that she was probably about to lose her job. But she could not get hold of her, all weekend.

On Monday morning, Kate was waiting at the gate for Janet.

Finally, Janet came in....

As best as she could, Kate told Janet that she would be interviewed immediately, and that she was almost certainly going to lose her job.

Janet was distraught. She had been away for the weekend abroad and had had her mobile phone switched off.

There was no way out.

She was interviewed. She admitted to having left the camera on a table. She could not defend this, and they had the evidence, because they had the photograph taken by one of her students.

She was asked to leave, immediately. Kate took her to the café across the road, but there was nothing either of them could do.

Another day, another Security problem. An Art teacher again, Len. Theirs was the most security-conscious job, as they used tools for the art work. And they had a shadow board in the classroom which was carefully monitored, but to all intents and purposes, it was an area which could lead to security problems.

One morning, the administrator rang Kate to say that the key to the Shadow Board was missing.

Missing? Kate's heart missed a beat. The tools in there were really dangerous if they fell into the wrong hands...large and small scissors, Stanley knives, scrapers, files...

Len did not work that day.

They tried to ring him, but he was not at home.

They searched and searched...Nothing.

She went to Oscar 1 and cancelled the Art that morning. No one was allowed into the Art Room.

She went to see Works, and without hesitating, they hurried to the Art Room, wrenched off the padlock and replaced it with a new one.

She rang her Governor and told him what had happened, and that she had secured the shadow cabinet.

It did not help. The phone turned blue as he expressed his feelings....

She assured him that she would keep looking for the keys, and he assured her that he would be speaking to her and to Len later.

They tried everything. The administrator was sure that Len had checked the shadow board, because he had signed that it was safe. She was almost sure that he had hung the keys in the key cabinet, but she wondered if he had left them on her desk, near the cabinet, and that they had fallen into her handbag. A handbag she had not brought into work.

She went home, to check her other handbag.

Kate continued to ring Len.

The key was not in the administrator's other handbag.

They searched the whole office, the staff room and the Art Room. No luck.

Finally, towards the end of the afternoon, Len answered his phone.

"The key...? The key to the Shadow Board...He did not have it, because he always replaced it at the end of the lesson."

He was just going to check his bag....

The key was there.

He managed to "get away" with a written warning, but he was lucky, as taking a key home from the department was very serious.

So, the missing scissors were not going to be much of a problem then?

Kate came into work early the next morning, dreading the inevitable interview. One of her teachers, Edward, was already at work.

"God, Kate, I forgot the scissors yesterday...I remembered that I hadn't put them back halfway through the night."

"Oh dear," Kate wanted to scream, but didn't...

"I'd kept them "safe", while I was using them, at the back of my pigeon hole, and then I forgot to put them back in the drawer...but here they are..."

"Oh dear," she said again, "we are both due for an interview with Security this morning. Oh dear," she repeated.

"Will I lose my job?" Ed was concerned.

"Not if I can help it." He was a good teacher, but at this moment, she was just slightly, very slightly, upset, to say the least. "But, do you know the trouble I've had? I couldn't find them last night...I had to report them missing...I had to see the Security Governor...I searched the place, but not the pigeon holes, because I did not think that anyone would be..."

"Kate, I'm sorry, I'm so sorry. Yes, how absolutely stupid of me." He was devastated. "What do we do now?"

"The prisoners' cells were probably checked last night...it meant a search...it meant that the officers probably had to go home late...I went home late..."

"Oh Kate...what can I say?"

"Well at least you will never again forget to replace the scissors."

He did not have to, as they were confiscated. Neither was sacked, but it was not the most pleasant of interviews. What is more, they were not the most popular of departments for a while. The prison rumours were rife...Education were giving out scissors, and all manner of tools, just like that...no security awareness...these civilians...hmmm...no security awareness.

She hadn't slept all night. Oh yes, Education was one of the most security aware, but that made no difference for the next few weeks.

She defended her department as best as she could, when she heard the rumours, however, there were always those rumours that she hadn't heard and was unable to defend.

There is always one question asked at all interviews for prison jobs:

"What is the most important issue in a prison?"

If the interviewee doesn't know the answer then he or she may forget the rest of the interview...

SECURITY! SECURITY!

Moving

After bereavement and divorce, moving is supposed to be the most stressful experience in life. Anyone who has moved will agree.

Moving in a prison is something else. It is not only a stressful experience, but it is close to what may be described as moving into and within Dante's hell. Although, there are many hands, few are secure and trustworthy.

Kate had her usual meeting with her Governor:

"I have a surprise for you," he said, "G1 education is now ready, so you can move in."

"Move in, when?"

"As soon as possible".

"Yes, but there are no shelves up, nothing is cleared. G1 has to be ready, absolutely ready."

"It will be, don't worry. You can start moving next week. Shut down Education for a week."

OK. This is a move from G3 to G1. This is a move which will involve moving desks, chairs, filing cabinets, posters, books, stationery, computers, art stuff, resources, and so on and so on.

The things in G3 need to be emptied, packed, then transported across, down to G1, unpacked and reassembled.

There are no lifts in the prison, and only a few prisoners are allowed outside. Most of the things will be carried down two flights of stairs by the prisoners themselves. There will then be two gates to be unlocked and locked each time.

Everything will need to be transported down a wing into G1. If you have a crew of ten prisoners, each carrying a box of books, they will have to gather round the gates of G3 Education, be unlocked out into the staircase, carry their things down the two flights of stairs, then gather again, at the gates into G1, wait for someone to unlock the gates, move through the gates, then the person who is unlocking and locking will need to catch them up quickly as they stride down the wing, because they cannot move in the prison without an escort. Along the way, the prisoners in the wing will try to steal as much as they can from the packages carried, then the carrying prisoners will have to wait at the gates of G1, so that the escort will unlock and lock the gates into G1....all the time counting and re-counting to make sure that there are still ten prisoners, and that one or more has not disappeared into the wing to see his friends. No pressure then.

Kate goes to see G1 Education on Friday afternoon. It used to be the RC Chapel, which has been used recently for Legal Visits. She finds, that despite being told that all will be clear, that is not the case. In the old office, there is much rubbish, and the walls have not been painted. There is an old organ, some chairs, hymn books. They cannot move the things from G3 until this lot has been cleared away.

She goes to fetch some green uniforms from "Stores" ready for the cleaners and painters on Monday.

On Monday, she leaves her deputy to start packing up the things in G3. The plan is that each teacher will pack his or her resources from the filing cabinets, escort his or her students to G1 with the resources and filing cabinets, then start unpacking at the other end. As the teachers work on different days, obviously the Monday teachers will start first, until they get through the whole week. However, it is clear now that the Monday teachers cannot move in until G1 has been cleaned and painted.

In G1, the prisoners carry out the rubbish through the outside door, and leave it in the outside world. The outside world here isn't really the outside world as there are still many gates to pass before the real outside world, but nevertheless, it is outside in the fresh air. And when we say prisoners carry out... Kate has to make sure that only the ones who have been banded to go outside can go outside. It is a feat of organisation. She stays at the outside gates supervising the rubbish eviction, which takes most of Monday. At least by the end of Monday, there is no more rubbish in G1.

This, of course means however, that the Monday teachers are going to have to leave their resources and filing cabinets for the Tuesday teachers.

There is also the matter of painting the offices, which will probably take most of Tuesday, which of course means that the Wednesday teachers will now be left with supervising Monday's and Tuesday's resources, and their own. Kate stays calm. Some of the more anxious teachers do not. Kate calms them. It will be finished. They will be moved. Everything will be all right in the end. On Friday they will be laughing in brand new classrooms. Beneath her calm, Kate wonders if she has descended into some fantasy parallel universe, and there will never be an end to this to-ing and fro-ing and moving, and shouting instructions, and shouting warnings, and shouting encouragement, and unlocking and locking gates, and watching the stationery, boxes of which are disappearing as she speaks, and supervising prisoners, and, and, and...she will laugh about this at a dinner party one day, she tries to reassure herself.

On Tuesday, she is told that the rubbish outside the Education Department cannot stay there. It has to be moved into big skips on the other side of the prison. OK.

She picks some "secure" prisoners and takes them across the prison, to the Main Stores, to fetch trolleys. She collects two trolleys, and the prisoners trolley them back around the inside of the outside walls. Then through a gate and into the passageway to the outside of G1 Education. Only the trolleys will not go round the rather tight bend in the passageway....Hmmmm. The prisoners shunt them back and forth, but there is no way on this earth that they will turn in such a tight space.

OK, they go back out through the gate, shunt the trolleys to the next gate, then into the "dungeons". Kate calls them "dungeons" because they are corridors which go under the prison. One of these corridors comes out just by G1 Education. It is really very dark here. The lights go on automatically as you walk, however, the corridors go off at all angles, and it is difficult to know whether you are walking down the correct one, until you find yourself coming out into the wrong part of the prison.

The trolley shunters shunt the trolleys along the "dungeon" corridors. Miraculously they and Kate do not wander off down the wrong corridor, and miraculously they do find their way into the courtyard outside G1.

So, Tuesday is filled with the painters painting supervised by some of the teachers, and the shunters shunting the rubbish around the prison, in trolleys, supervised by Kate.

By the end of Tuesday, Kate is so tired that she can hardly stand.

Finally, on Wednesday, they start moving the actual furniture and resources from G3. The big teachers' desks...Oh dear. The corridors in G1 Education are so narrow that when they try to get the desks into the classrooms and the offices, they cannot turn the desks in through the doors. They try turning them sideways, at angles, pushing, pulling....nothing works....it's just not going to happen.

Kate decides that they will have to be taken apart and reassembled inside. They have no tools to do this and certainly if they did have, the prisoners would not be trusted with them.

Kate goes to the Works Department to borrow their electric drill. The desks will have to be disassembled and reassembled by the teachers themselves during the lunch break.

On Wednesday afternoon, she goes across to see how the administrator is managing with packing all the things from the office. She finds him sitting in the office. Nothing has been done, and he is looking extremely pale. He has a heart condition. Oh my God...Don't move... Don't touch anything...Kate is worried. The poor man has not been employed to pack and move heavy things. He will need to sit and supervise, and she will pack the things in the office. Obviously, the prisoners will not be allowed to help, as there is much classified information in the things stored. Most of these things will have to be moved by the teachers themselves.

Thursday seems to be a day of frenzied packing, moving, carrying, shunting, packing, moving, carrying, shunting...Unpacking, unpacking, unpacking, storing, unpacking. Then smiling, smiling, smiling...hysterically. Were they all going to go mad by Friday, Kate wondered? She wouldn't be surprised.

At last, everything has been moved across. Kate goes for a final look at the old Education Department. It looks very sad. There is rubbish strewn around the floors. Old posters have been left behind. Shelves are empty, classrooms are empty. There is such an emptiness, and only "ghosts" are left behind...This is where...and this is where...

There is still much to do in the new Department, but they will be opening for lessons on Monday.

On Friday the staff are trying to cram more things into the classrooms, drawers and filing cabinets, and the new shelves and whiteboards are going up as promised. Kate makes a few more trips to the skip and then by the end of the day...they decide to leave it and go for a drink.

Everyone has lost the will to live, but no one is actually dead from exhaustion yet. Kate feels that the last week has been a nightmare, but they moved. There were times when she thought that they might still be moving next year. There were times when she thought they would all end up in a "nice rest home for hysterical teachers and Head". There were times when she thought she might get lost in the "dungeon" corridors beneath the prison, ferrying and shunting trolleys for the rest of her life. And there were times when she thought that they would end up in a Greek Tragedy, killing each other and their students...

So at least, they were all still alive and ready to enjoy a lovely big glass of whatever...and laughing and laughing, as they recalled some of the horror stories of the week. She knew they would be laughing in the end...they always did.

Dyslexia

A captive audience! Hmmmm.

To find anyone in a prison is not as easy as you think.

Firstly, it is a huge place and there are a lot of prisoners, about 1150 of them.

Secondly, there may be a hundred and one places the prisoner has been taken to.

The system is simple and generally works very well. Prisoners are on an unlocking list for various activities. So, a prisoner, for example, who is in Education will be on the Education Unlocking list. He will be unlocked at about 7.45 in the morning, and at about 8.30, he will gather with others for Education at his wing gates. The officers at these gates will check their lists and the prisoner will begin making his way towards the Education Department in its wing. At the gates of the department, he will be checked again by the Education administrator and if on the list, he will be allowed into the department. At 8.45 the gates will be locked, and the administrator will count the numbers from each wing and phone the information to the Centre. In the meantime, the wings will have sent their own information, i.e. the numbers that they have sent to Education, and hopefully, the two tally.

If, however, the prisoner has decided to make a detour to see his mates in the wing housing the Education Department, the numbers do not tally. He will not want to be in this situation, as it does not make him very popular, so unpopular in fact that he may be put on report, so he will generally bang and knock on the Education Department's doors as soon as possible, and make up some excuse for why he is late. He may be fortunate and get in if he's only a few minutes late and the numbers have not gone through. He may be "unfortunate" and get into trouble.

When Kate used to do the Dyslexia assessing, she worked from a list of those who have been referred to her either by the wing or the teachers, who may or may not be dyslexic. She would need to wait in the morning until the roll is correct, in other words until the wing and activity numbers tally, and then would set off to find the prisoners she needed to see. The wings spread out from the Centre. A to the left, with B behind it, then C and D bearing left, E straight ahead, then G to the right. Each wing has five landings. A prisoner's location is classified by his wing, landing and cell number. So Smith PB9595 might be in D531, i.e., in D Wing on the 5th landing in cell 31. It is always sod's law that the prisoner she has to see is on the highest landing and the furthest from Education. And there are many gates to unlock and lock between the Education department and her goal.

The usual pattern was that Kate found the prisoner's location on the prison database, LIDS. So, Smith PB9595, in D531. She walked to D wing, up the five flights of stairs to the fifth landing and to cell 31.

Invariably…empty.

If they were on association, and outside their cells, she would ask the prisoners nearby whether they knew off-hand where Mr. Smith could be. For some reason, everyone in the prison usually assumed that anyone and everyone had gone to Education.

"Smithy? – He's on Education."

"No he isn't, because that's where I've just come from."

So, to the Wing Office.

"Smith, PB 9595? He's on Education."

"No, he isn't because I……"

"Oh no, he's in the Gym."

Now Gym is a way away. So Kate would trail to the Gym.

"Jack Smith, he's not here, he's probably in Education."

"Nooo, he isn't in Education…."

"Maybe he has a visit."

So Kate would trail down to the Visits, back near Education…"

"No, he has no visit today. I bet he's in……Ed…."

"Noooo!….

"Oh, he's probably still in his wing then."

Back in his wing again and after the prisoners have shouted, Smith…. Smithy…. Lady wants you….he will emerge from his mate's cell, and finally, finally, finally, Kate has him. But as an assessment takes about an hour, she will have wasted her precious assessment hour just trying to find him.

It was a precious hour because so much emerged from these Dyslexia Assessments. Prisoners often cried, because they had had such a difficult time not understanding why they had not been able to learn. They would often tell Kate horrendous stories about their life, show wounds from beatings, from neglect, even from cigarette burns. Not all prisoners come from a "poor" background, and not all are neglected even if they do, but so many of them come from dysfunctional families, where education was the last priority, and either mum or dad or both were on drugs, or on alcohol, or were just unable to cope with the daily grind. This does not excuse the ones whose lifestyle is centred around "dodging the system", or not having a system to dodge, because they have been outside any system, particularly if they had been "inside", but the stories were still often unbearable to hear. The prisoners generally have few aspirations, but some want immediate gratification, and Kate doesn't know who to blame, if anyone. Some live only for the next fix, and do everything, even steal from their grandmothers to get that fix. Drugs are the biggest problem in their society, as in all societies, but with a very limited income, they rely on stealing and robbing for the drugs that they use. This leads them on a downward spiral, towards prison, disease, and possibly death. Their "friends" and "acquaintances" are also in the same spiral, and so each one feeds off the misery of this existence and each other, because a life where addiction and danger are ever present seems to be the only life they know. Depressing, and endless. As a dyslexia assessor and Education Manager, Kate, like the other teachers, can see the reasons, but not the solutions, if there are any.

There are two tests for dyslexia, one, a short one, shows if there is an indication of dyslexia , and the other a full assessment.

To check, Kate would give the student a reading test, a dictation and a free writing exercise, then ask him a number of questions. Most adults have visual dyslexia, which is indicated by the dyslexic reading a passage often perfectly, but not knowing what he has read about, and therefore having to read it all over again.... and again. His writing will be completely phonetic, because he has no visual memory and so has to spell the word as if from new every time. This means that he has to rely, not on his visual memory as the rest of us do, but on spelling out the word phonetically, which as we all know, is not at all a reliable way of spelling in the English language, and what is more, very ponderous. He may have had hearing problems as a child. He will almost certainly not have been helped at school, or if he was, he would have been sent to the special unit, which was for the "dunces" as everyone at school knew, and possibly labelled as lazy or stupid. If he wasn't labelled stupid, he would have applied that label to himself, because according to his "diagnosis" there could be no other reason why he could not "capture" the magic of reading and writing. Without visual memory, he would have had difficulty copying, particularly from the board, as he would have to copy a word letter by letter. His inability to remember words would mean that his creative writing was often very good, but, because he would spend an awful lot of time trying to work out how to spell the words, would be hindered. His attempts therefore at creative writing were usually simplistic and boring, because he used words which were simple and boring but easy to memorise. He may also have sequencing problems and so forget the order of things like the alphabet, and months, or phone numbers in the right order, which could mean that he did not get to where he should have been, when he should have. He would have short-term memory difficulties, which would also affect his learning and ability to cope. He may have spatial/temporal problems, particularly left/right confusion, get lost easily, and find it difficult to tell the time, and motor problems which would be indicated by his awkwardness when writing.

He would however, be very good at being creative, especially when working with practical subjects. So his best subjects at school may have been art, drama, carpentry, woodwork, metalwork, etc etc. And he would almost certainly have found ways to try to beat his problems with dyslexia in the most ingenious, inventive and resourceful ways, because being dyslexic has not the slightest link to intelligence.

Kate had been trained as an assessor in 1990, and her first student was Jack.

Jack had been on her Basic Skills class. He was bright, sensible, and clearly thirsting for knowledge, but "lazy".

"Jack, have you read that book I gave you?"

"No, Miss, it's too hard."

"Don't be silly, it can't be too hard."

"Have you done that comprehension?"

"No, Miss, I can't do comprehensions."

"Don't be silly, of course you can. Why are you always so difficult?"

She was trying to prepare him for the English exams and it seemed hopeless to her.

She was interested in Dyslexia in adults, and had a vague preconception of what dyslexia meant – people couldn't read and they couldn't write. They had bad memories. But really she knew little else. She had persuaded her Manager to allow her to go on a course, and she was due to go to her first session.

Horrors! Right at the beginning of the first session, they looked at some of the indicators of dyslexia....an inability to understand what you read, and an inability to spell...Could Jack be dyslexic? But he could read, and he could write, just not write correctly....But he said that he found it hard to read, but he *could* read, so what did that mean?

When she went back to the prison...

"Jack, God almighty, I think you might be dyslexic."

"Miss, don't be silly, I can read and write."

Little by little, week by week, Kate began to realise that everything pointed to Jack being dyslexic.

"So, when you read, you read perfectly, why can't you understand what you read?"

"Because, I just seem to get to the bottom of the page, and nothing has made sense, and I can't remember anything. I lose my place and get confused about where I've got to, then I try to make up what I think I've read, because I do remember some of the words, but it's such a drag, Miss, that even if I want to read something so badly, I can't face reading, as…"

"So, it's really frustrating for you…Oh Jack. I'm so sorry…How awful…"

Gradually, she realised that Jack focused on each word as he read, rather than skim, and when he tried to do that, it was soon evident that he was not focused on the meaning and lost the meaning, and had to read from the beginning again. Frustrating was not the word. What a terrible thing, when reading was one of the great pleasures of life.

"What if you underline the first sentence in the paragraph, read that one twice, so that you know what may be coming next?"

"OK, Miss, I'll give it a go."

It was hard. Spelling would be learnt again and again, then forgotten the next day.

They would practise together.

"So, what's that first sentence about, Jack? So what will the paragraph be about?"

They concentrated on stuff Jack really enjoyed, and Kate brought in John Romer's books on history and philosophy, which Jack painstakingly "ploughed" through and enjoyed.

In her department now, they have a computer programme to help, and four teachers with expertise to help. Then, they could only try out strategies that might or might not help Jack.

But the main, the biggest, the greatest achievement was the tremendous growth in Jack's belief in himself. From someone who had thought that he was stupid and lazy and ineffectual, Jack could now see himself as an intelligent and cultured, interesting human being…and that was huge.

Then BBC2 approached the prison as they were making a documentary about Dyslexia and prisons, using new information being researched in the US. Kate was one of the very few prison teachers at the time to have had training in Dyslexia assessment, so obviously she was the first choice to take part in this documentary.

Although she was assured that the documentary did not indicate that criminality was linked to dyslexia in any way, Kate was dubious. She knew from past experience how clever editing could completely misconstrue a sentence or an opinion. She wanted however, to have a chance to talk about dyslexia, as she had become very passionate about it.

In the end, she decided that she would not take part, but that Jack could, if he wanted to, and his participation would probably be more significant than hers.

Jack was happy to take part.

Kate still cries when she remembers Jack and that documentary, and not much makes her cry.

The end… the end is a killer. Jack talks about his dyslexia and how he and Kate have tried to beat his problems with reading and spelling. He talks about his growing self-esteem, and his pursuit in his knowledge. He had always believed that his IQ must be very low as he couldn't function properly with the written word, but now he knows that that is untrue, and that he is intelligent, and therefore able to hold his own anywhere with anything.

It ends...it ends...with the interviewer asking Jack, what changed when he was diagnosed a dyslexic?

He hesitates for a long, long time, giving it much thought...then he says:

"Everything...."

After the documentary Kate was asked to go to the House of Lords to speak on behalf of prisoners with dyslexia.

She was so excited.   This was her chance to tell these influential people about dyslexia.   At last she would have a voice which mattered.

When she arrived, she was taken to a room somewhere in the Houses of Parliament.   She had no idea where, as it was all such a maze.   As she walked, she became more and more overwhelmed by the sheer grandeur of the place, so that by the time she arrived for the discussion about dyslexia, she had been so overwhelmed that she was speechless.   The room was grand.   The walls were covered in tapestries.   The chairs were like little thrones, and sitting on them were people with the familiar faces of some of the Lords she knew from the media. With them were governors, probation officers, heads of this and heads of that, anyone who was anyone in the prison service seemed to have gathered here to talk about Dyslexia and talk they did, very eloquently and very convincingly, which was good.   But...her contribution....?

Oh my God, she was thinking as the discussion continued. It knocked her theory that knowledge was power right down the drain.   She probably knew more about dyslexia than any of them put together, but with such an assembly of power, her knowledge was not going to help.   So much so, that when she was asked to speak, as the one person who knew, *really knew* about dyslexia in prison she couldn't. She got up, smiled shyly and told them that everything that they had said was true, that she agreed with everything they had said and that there needed to be more work done in prisons as for various reasons, none to do with any tendency towards criminality, there were more dyslexics in prison than on the outside. So much for her great contribution at the House of Lords.

However, even if wheels grind slowly, they grind...

In 1998, the British Dyslexia Association funded a support programme in the prison for dyslexics. It was based on multi-sensory help. Obviously, if one of the particular senses, such as visual perception, had become impaired by a dyslexic tendency, you could use other senses, such as touch on a computer, to support learning. And a computer had various techniques to aid writing and spelling, besides displaying writing which was clear, correct and therefore easier to memorise. What is more, as the programme was designed for computers, and work from computers allowed dyslexics individual help and complete control over their learning, it meant that dyslexics could support themselves at their own pace, in their own time and without fear of any embarrassment, thus increasing their self-esteem at the same time as helping with spelling and reading. It was such a success that even the Prime Minister, Tony Blair came to see it. And for Kate it meant that, although the Dyslexic support teacher was certainly not redundant, she had some support beyond her own inventive techniques.

Kate had become known as one of the specialists in Dyslexia in adults in prison.

She was in a book shop one day, and was looking for a recently published book on Adult Dyslexia. She found the book and turned to the Index. Her name jumped out from the book. Her name! She went up to the cash desk and pointed this out to the lady there. Not impressed at all.

"But my name, my name is in a book," she gabbled.

"Well, are you going to buy it or not?"

So her claim to fame…well ……

Gradually, work with Dyslexics became almost a mainstay in prisons across the country and despite it not being completely achieved, Kate knew that this was what she had always hoped for. A lot had been achieved since those first days when she was one of the few….Now, a prisoner diagnosed with dyslexia had an explanation, had a reason for his problems, and so he no longer felt stupid, or lazy or ineffectual.

He would be sent to a Dyslexia Support class and there find support for his difficulties with the written word.

Yes, indeed, *everything* had changed.

The Royal Visit

There were always visitors to the Education Department, actors, musicians, poets, writers, pop stars, DJs and Kate, the Education Manager, was always pleasantly surprised at how very charming and very polite they all were. Surprised, because for some reason, she always expected celebrities to have big egos, isn't that what was always written about them? She realised quickly, soon after she had become the Manager, that these were ordinary people who had to live in a world of extraordinary competition, and that like good "products", which many of them had become through no fault of their own, they had to "sell" and "market" themselves. Who they were to the world, was not who they truly were. Theirs was a world where even the clothes on their backs had to make a statement, and what they said and what they did would be publicity, good or bad. No, everyone she had ever met who was in the public eye had been absolutely lovely.

When they were doing a production of Macbeth in the prison, the visiting professional actors taking part had been wearing prison uniforms, so you could not distinguish them from the prisoners. At the first performance to the prisoners, she had asked one of her students in the audience to hold a place for her while she went to greet the visiting actors. She came up to them, and asked, as they were dressed like prisoners, if they were actors or prisoners? A joke. One of them had replied, in the best luvvy tradition, that, " we are all prisoners in some way..." Kate hurried back to her normal prisoners, and asked if she could vomit into their laps. But that was cruel. The actor was trying to be respectful about the prisoners and trying to show that he was not fazed at being surrounded by them and if he'd only known how condescending and precious he sounded, he would not have made that comment. Still, it was easy for Kate, she had worked in the place for ever.

Then, the big one.

A Royal visit.

Princess Anne was coming to open a special unit in the prison, where various departments, catering for all the prisoners' problems, would be under one roof, in one giant office. This would mean that you would not need to wander around the huge prison to sort out housing, bail, ROTL, Transfers, Legal matters, etc., etc., but could do it all, if needed, in one "fell swoop".

After the opening, the Princess would be visiting D Wing Education Department. The department had been told by the Governor that he would escort her down D Wing, where all the teaching staff would be lined up in front of the department. Kate would then introduce the Princess to her staff, take her into the department and show her how it worked.

She would say, "Your Royal Highness," curtsy, then say, "may I introduce my staff...." No prepared formula there, you notice.

Then came the nerves. If Princess Anne knew how nervous the public get at meeting Royalty, she would probably laugh. Kate was worried that she would:

1.   Forget to curtsy.

2.   Forget to call the Princess 'Your Royal Highness'.

3.   Forget the teachers' names.

4.   Forget the students' names.

5.   Forget what went on in her department and so talk nonsense to the Princess, thus illustrating her "excellence" at her job.

6. Forget everything and have done with it.

First came the important discussions of who would meet her and where, how the classes were to be presented and the great clean. She was not going to see any rubbish in this Education Department.

For instance, there was a lengthy, but "*important*" discussion about whether the Dyslexia Support students would continue with their work at the computers, which would mean that they would continue sitting down when the Princess came into the classroom, which was not at all respectful, or whether they should stop working and stand up to welcome her, which was respectful but which caused the problem of what to do then; sit down immediately and start working again at the computers; sit down only when the Princess asked to be shown something on the computer; or not sit down at all and stand up to do everything, even if it looked ridiculous. No, these were important points to Kate! The Governor hadn't selected the Education Department to be presented to Her Highness, only to be embarrassed by people jumping up and down like yo-yos, and seemingly to show little respect.

Then, the prisoners:

"Miss, can I tell her about my appeal? The judge ain't really all there, Miss, can I tell her?"

"If you so much as mention an appeal, or anything else, and that goes for the rest of you...I will hang you upside down over a slow fire....You will welcome her properly, as you know how. You will not, I repeat *not* make her think that we are a bunch of idiots in this department."

"Yep, but she should know..."

"You just dare.... I'm warning you all."

The morning of the visit.

If Kate practised the curtsy once.....she practised it a hundred times.   In   the   staffroom...   "Do   I   look   OK?"...In   the classrooms, "Do I look OK?" Only the students also got a sermon...   "Now, you won't forget to be welcoming. Now, you won't forget to stand up, and greet her as you should".

"Yes, Miss, yes, Miss...No, Miss, no Miss.....Don't worry."

"Yes, but is this OK?" Kate was certain that by the end of the visit, the students and the staff were ready to hang *her* over a slow fire.

"Now if I forget your name, and I might, in all the fluster, will you just pretend that your name is what I call you?"

Then,   they   were   standing   there.   The   corridor   in   the department was sparkling. The classrooms looked like new. There were bright new posters up. The prisoners were busy, their teachers looked professional (as always – a brilliant staff).

Kate was standing with the teachers who were not in the classroom. They were in a line ready to greet the princess. Kate reminded herself for the one hundred millionth time that she was to wait until the Governor introduced her, then to curtsy, say her bit, then not call her Royal Highness again, but Ma'am.

Ready? As they would ever be.

She was coming towards them down the wide D1 Wing. She was tiny, very slim. There was a bright smile on her face.

She came up to Kate. The curtsy...perfect, she hadn't fallen over... "Your Royal Highness, may I present my staff...." She introduced them one by one and got all their names right.

The Princess smiled and smiled. She stepped into the centre of the assembly of staff and said,

"Come round, come round, let me talk to you." She asked them why they had elected to work in prison, what interested them in the work, and then moved to the door of the department.

In the Dyslexia Room, the students were busy working at the computers. Sitting! She went round quietly asking them what they were doing, how they were doing. She tried out some exercises with them. She was great. How boring for her, but she showed no sign of boredom. She was brilliant.

Then Kate took her to the ESOL (English for Speakers of Other Languages) class. The class stood up as she walked in. The Italians chanted, "Good Morning, Principessa", the others muttered something...but it all sounded good.

She asked them about how they learnt the English language. She told them that she had been sent to France to do nothing but learn French...She laughed to Kate, and asked if she had learnt Latin, and both Princess and Manager grumbled at the declensions. Kate forgot to call her ma'am, in fact after the initial great flourish, and the Your Highness, Kate didn't call the Princess anything. Hmmmmm....

Then she left.

The place erupted. Lucky she hadn't popped back, because everyone was so relieved that they were laughing insanely and if she had walked in then, she would have wondered what the Government was doing about the crazy teachers who were working in British prisons.

The prisoners too were proud of themselves, and as bad as the staff. She was lovely, wasn't she? How professional. Never looked bored once, must have been, must have been so bored, my God.

"She spoke to me Miss...she spoke to me..."

"What did she say?....what did she say?....And what did you say to that…yes, that's good. Good answer…."

"Well done, everyone, well done…"

They had done well…

The Concert

She had "done her time" and decided that she would retire.

Kate had thought and thought about her decision, and how much she would miss the prisoners and her staff, but after thirty seven years, she thought that the time had come for a rest.

During a concert to celebrate Black History Month in October, she realised that this would probably be her last concert in the prison.

Sadly, she walked along the "fives", on the fifth floor, towards her office, and as usual stopped to chat to her neighbours, the prisoners whose cells were there.

"Oh, guys, what a wonderful concert. You were great...absolutely fantastic. So enjoyed it....It will probably be my last concert...I've decided to retire."

"Miss, Miss, hey...retire?"

"Would you like us to prepare a concert for you when you go, Miss?" said Edward, the Race Relations Rep.

"A concert, for when I go...that would be wonderful. But I won't be going till March..."

And that was that...Her last concert.

Christmas came and went. An Inspection was due in April and Kate did not think again about the concert. The teachers were too busy, and the prisoners would have forgotten.

Gradually, she packed and was quite proud of the fact that she managed to get her "belongings" after thirty seven years into two boxes. She had to be ruthless, and she was. She was not taking any memories, only the essential things she may need "on the out".

Her farewell party came and went and her last day at work, Monday, was drawing ever nearer. The Governor had been to see her to thank her, and oddly he said that he was sorry that he could not be there on Monday. Could be where? Of course... there would be some sort of meeting in one of the classrooms, she supposed, when the Deputies would make a speech, and that would be that...

On Monday at lunchtime, she noticed that staff were coming in who were not usually in on a Monday... Yes, there would be some little presentation.

She was doing some last-minute work on her computer with the Operations Manager from the college, and so when the phone went and the Manager went to answer it, Kate realised that the place was empty.

"OK, we're going over to Education..." said her colleague. "Go and put on some make up."

"Why, what's going to happen?" Kate asked, but knew already.

They both hurried along the wings to the Education Department.

When she got to the gates, and was about to go in, her colleague pulled her away...

"No, we're off to the Sports Hall upstairs."

"Oh God," Kate wondered what was happening. "What's in there?"

"Let's go and see..."

There they all were. Students on chairs in the centre and staff around the walls.

Kate began to feel that this was unreal, that it was some sort of dream.

A Governor asked her up to the front and presented her with a huge bouquet...and then....the concert.

A concert! They had prepared a concert. But how? When? She had heard no rehearsals. Not seen anyone creeping around looking sheepish. Nor anyone seemingly caught doing something they were hiding from her.

A concert! And what a concert. She couldn't cry, and anyway, she was too taken aback and mesmerised by what was happening to feel that this was real. What a wonderful, wonderful surprise. What a wonderful way to finish off her thirty seven years.

First the teachers...they had formed a choir... A choir?...When? How? She laughed with the sheer joy of it, and whatever any critic may have said if they were asked to judge, to Kate this choir was fantastic, the best in the world.

Then students...many had written poems to her and about her. Each read his poem. Some of the teachers too had written Odes to Kate.

Then the students again, music this time...wonderful, exciting, buzzing music. Her heart sang too. Oh, how kind they were.

Edward grinned at her...."You thought we'd forgotten, well...we promised..." This time it was difficult to hold back the tears... One of the students was singing in Punjabi above the others' rapping and over a background of guitars and drums, so unusual, and amazing...they had created a completely new sound. For a second she thought that this must be pursued, and that she would explore how they could export this sound, for the self-esteem of the students who had created it...and then, she realised that she was no longer the Manager, and that there would be no more pursuing, developing, creating, organising or anything which had made her life so exciting for the last thirty seven years.

Exciting it had been...

How would she manage without these wonderful people?

Lightning Source UK Ltd.
Milton Keynes UK
07 January 2011
165322UK00001B/16/P